SUSAN A JENNINGS

Ruins in Silk

Double Prequel to ... The Sophie's War Novels & The Blue Pendant

SaRaKa InPrint

THIS BOOK WAS WRITTEN IN ENGLISH CANADIAN STYLE WITH CANADIAN SPELLING. AMERICAN AND BRITISH READERS MAY NOTICE SOME DIFFERENCES IN THE SPELLING.

Second edition

ISBN: 978-1-989553-27-5

Editing by Meghan Negrijn

This book was professionally typeset on Reedsy.
Find out more at reedsy.com

This second edition has a very special dedication to recognize some wonderful people who came into my life through my late mother, Betty Jennings.
With the warmest thanks and much love

I dedicate this book to
Helen Collette
Julia Munro
Lesley Johnson

Three amazing women who befriended, entertained and cared for my late mother and befriend me during those difficult months after she passed away.
Three wonderful friends
Thank you!

Contents

Preface

An Introduction

The Romano brothers were silkworm farmers, as was their father, grandfather, and several generations of great-grandfathers before them. Sericulture, the cultivation of silkworms, is a delicate process, demanding precise conditions and specialized knowledge. The white mulberry tree, the only food source for silkworms, requires an especially fertile soil, a specific elevation and many hours of bright sunshine. These conditions are imperative for the tree to produce the copious amount of mulberry leaves needed for the silkworms' insatiable appetites as they form their silk cocoons. The Romanos' silk farm in Lucca in northern Italy was perfectly situated for sericulture, and sericulture pumped through the brothers' veins.

Roberto, the younger of the two, had a passion for sericulture that bordered on obsessive. He tended the delicate silkworms with such tenacity that the end result was a fine silk thread. The Romanos had supplied the Bologna Silk Mill—famous for a particularly fine veil silk fabric—for generations.

Alberto, although well versed in the art of sericulture, had little interest in the hands-on aspect of farming. His passion was the business, not only for profit but also the challenge of expanding the Romano name and growing new markets outside Europe. He recognized that supplying only one silk manufacturer would not sustain the silk farm in 1906.

Establishing a Romano silk mill and expanding the business close to home was Alberto's first goal. Over recent years, conducting business in Italy and France had become overly competitive. The price of raw silk had been reduced to a fraction of its worth, causing corruption among the silk producers and buyers. Alberto loathed dishonesty and he wasn't comfortable competing against his own customer in Bologna. He expanded his search beyond the shores of Europe and found a ready market in Britain among the Victorian and Edwardian mindset of the upper and middle classes.

The Romanos purchased and refurbished an old textile mill in Derby, in the Midlands of England. It would accommodate silk spinning and weaving. The Lombes Mill, its origins dating back to the thriving silk industry of the 17th century, was now the Romano Silk Mill.

The brothers split up. Roberto and his wife, Maria, remained in Italy, managing the silk farm and producing the raw silk. Alberto and his wife, Martina, and daughter, Sophie, moved to Derby to spin and weave the Romano silk for British high society.

September 1906 – Italy to England

The Lucca train station was crowded. Two tall handsome men stood confidently above the crowd. They were almost identical in looks and stature except for their clothing. One, a casual, almost peasant-like farmer, unloaded the trunks and bags onto the baggage cart. The other man, immaculately dressed in a dark suit, waistcoat and stiff white collar, unobtrusively tipped the porter. His wife slipped her arm under his, and his daughter held her mother's hand as they approached the train carriage.

Roberto kissed and hugged his niece, Sophie, and fondly kissed his sister-in-law, Martina, on each cheek and then helped them board the train. The brothers hugged and slapped each other on the back, shaking hands with a defiant resolve for success.

"Brother, it is up to you make our new venture in England prosper and our father and grandfathers proud." Roberto's words sounded enthusiastic to everyone except Alberto. He heard the edge of doubt in his brother's voice.

"Have faith, Roberto. Romano silk will become a household name. Derby is only the beginning. I've always had faith in your farming skills. The silkworms have no better guardian. Treat the business as well as you do the silkworms and the farm will thrive. I will do my job in England."

No one was more aware of the risks than Alberto. If either the farm or the Derby silk mill did not thrive, they risked losing it all. But to do nothing was certain death for the generations-old Romano Silk and Alberto would not let that happen. Pushing any doubts from his mind, he took his seat beside his wife. The train jerked a few times and then picked up speed. Alberto smiled at his little family as they began their journey to England and a bright future.

Twelve-year-old Sophie sat by the window, her eyes bright with excitement. "Papa, what is it like in England?"

"It's different. I think we'll miss the sunshine; I understand it rains daily in England. I have leased a big house with a big garden not far from the mill. Mama will enjoy the garden. The rain makes the plants grow." Alberto took his wife's hand. "You will like it once we've settled." Martina moved her lips, but instead of the intended smile her lips quivered and sadness trickled down her cheek. Alberto gently wiped her tears, making her smile.

"English gardens are pretty. It will be nice to tend to a variety of flowers. I shall enjoy sketching and painting in the garden. Art is good for the soul and my soul will draw strength to endure this new life."

"And so it will my dear." Alberto couldn't take his eyes off Martina. He wanted to kiss her and make her sadness go away. He felt guilty for asking her to leave Italy, particularly because he had not confided the true reason—sustaining the Romano name and business.

"You look pale, my dear. Are you feeling unwell?"

"A little nervous, that's all." Martina pulled the veil of her hat down to conceal her tears. Closing her eyes, she leaned her head against the seat. The soft, gold-coloured feathers on her hat moved delicately to the rhythm of the train. Alberto frowned. Martina looked so fragile. Her tight-fitting grey suit seemed to be all that prevented her from crumbling to the floor. He gently caressed her gloved hand and glancing towards Sophie, smiled reassuringly. He thought of his secret passion of passing on his legacy as his father and grandfathers had done before him. He regretted not having a son, but he had every intention that the Romano birthright would pass on to his daughter, Sophie.

The train sped towards Livorno, the seaport where they would board the ship for England. Martina's health declined after they'd set sail. Already nervous and unwell, the vessel's movement caused her great discomfort and bouts of seasickness. Afraid that she might die, Alberto called the ship's surgeon, who assured him that Martina would recover as soon as they arrived in England.

By the time they reached the hotel in London, Martina had to be carried to their room. Alberto, his face taut with anxiety, asked the hotel to call a physician. The doctor diagnosed a nervous disposition aggravated by the journey and prescribed laudanum to keep her calm and a tonic to build her strength. He advised them not to continue their journey to Derby for a few days.

* * *

The family arrived at Derby train station a week behind schedule. Martina leaned heavily on Alberto as they left the train and walked to the waiting carriage. She shivered slightly, glanced up at the dull, overcast sky and shivered again. Sophie jumped in and sat beside her mother. After arranging for the trunks to be sent separately, Alberto entered the carriage and tapped the roof with his cane. The horse's hooves sounded hollow on the road as the carriage moved forward on the final leg of their journey to Oak House.

Dalton and Mrs. Simpson—the butler and house-keeper—stood on the threshold of the front door. Cook and three maids lined up to greet their new master and mistress.

"Welcome to Oak House sir…madam." Dalton bowed stiffly at his waist. "Allow me to present the staff."

Alberto placed one hand on Martina's arm and held Sophie's hand with the other as they entered the hall nodding to the staff. Sophie was in awe of the young maids, all in black dresses with white frilly aprons and small lace caps on their heads. Cook wore a long white dress, white apron and white cap covering her head, wisps of brown hair escaped and brushed against her friendly, rosy cheeks. Mrs. Simpson wore a dark green dress buttoned to her chin with her skirts brushing the floor and her hair neatly rolled at the nape of her neck. Sophie wasn't sure about this severe looking lady and held her father's hand tightly. Dalton was equally imposing in his black suit, white shirt and stiff posture. She wondered if he had something wrong with his legs and had an intense desire to mimic his stilted walk but decided against it.

Martina nodded, but not having learned any English yet, she directed Italian words to Mrs. Simpson. Several awkward seconds passed and Martina's expression had become quite desperate.

"*La prego mi indichi la mia camera.*"

Troubled by Martina's shrill voice Alberto took her hand to calm her and spoke to Mrs Simpson. "My wife is asking you to take her to her room."

"Thank you, sir." Seeing Martina's grey complexion and the white handkerchief brush across her brow, Mrs. Simpson finally recognized her mistress's poor health, and led the way to the master bedroom.

"Madam, I hope the house is satisfactory. Perhaps you could offer some advice as to how you like things run?" Martina didn't answer. Mrs. Simpson frowned as her mistress swayed. "I'll send a maid to help you." Martina continued mopping the beads of perspiration from her brow.

Alarmed by her mistress's condition Mrs. Simpson asked, "Would madam like me to call the doctor?" Realizing Signora Romano didn't understand. She repeated her questions demonstrating with exaggerated arm movements. Finally, Signora Romano answered, "*Sì, mi mandi pure la cameriera, ma non necessito del dottore.*" Mrs. Simpson pulled the bell rope and waited for the maid. She'd had the foresight to hire one maid who spoke Italian. Content that the mistress of the house was being looked after, but somewhat exasperated that she had no instructions about meals or the duties expected of the staff, she went downstairs.

While Mrs. Simpson tended to Martina, Dalton had escorted Sophie and Alberto on a tour of the various family sitting rooms. Oak House was a Georgian mansion with many rooms filled with large ornate furniture. Sophie clung to her father's hand, sniffing at the funny smell and shivering at the dampness. She glanced suspiciously at the walls as they seemed to be closing in like a bad nightmare. Her excitement was waning as she could barely breathe. She thought about Italy: the spacious uncluttered rooms, bare wooden or cool ceramic floors and sunlight streaming through open windows with a constant breeze flowing through the house.

Then they had entered the study. Sophie liked this room. She released Alberto's hand and walked to the big window that overlooked a great expanse of green lawn, a rose garden, neat flowerbeds and a willow tree that swayed and dipped its branches into the river.

"Papa, look, there's a river at the end of the garden."

Alberto joined Sophie at the window. "That is the River Derwent and the building across the river is The Romano Silk Mill. Isn't it…" Mrs. Simpson's voice interrupted. "Excuse me sir! Your wife is unable to instruct me on how she would like the household to be run."

Annoyed at the intrusion, Alberto spoke sharply, making Mrs. Simpson recoil: "As housekeeper, I expect you to do what you are paid to do." He glanced towards Sophie, realizing the harshness of his words, and in a gentler tone, continued, "Do what you think is best. My wife will speak with you when she is feeling better."

"Yes, sir." Mrs. Simpson sighed as she left the room.

Dalton cleared his throat. "Sir, shall I bring some brandy? And what time shall I tell cook to serve dinner?"

"*Grazie.* Dinner at eight for me and have a tray sent up for my wife. Sophie can eat with me tonight."

Dalton handed Alberto a glass of brandy. "You must be hungry after your journey. I will have afternoon tea sent up." Dalton bent towards Sophie and she began to pull back but stopped, seeing kindness in his eyes. Behind that stiffness was a lovely smile. "And perhaps some cordial for Miss Sophie?" He straightened up, again addressing Alberto. "Sir, I don't believe Mrs. Simpson hired a governess for Miss Sophie."

"I'll speak to Signora Romano later. Sophie attends school, or did in Italy."

The cordial turned out to be a drink that tasted like strawberries. "Papa, this is the best drink I've ever tasted." She stared at the minute sandwiches, took two while eyeing her father and wondered if she was being greedy, but the pangs of hunger overruled. The sandwiches tasted good and she ate several. The cakes were even smaller. Her father picked up three at once, and she did the same. She caught her father's amused expression and they both started giggling.

"The English insist on being delicate, although I've never understood why. Sophie, remember that if we have guests for afternoon tea, it is polite to take one sandwich and one cake at a time. While there is just the two of us, let us enjoy the food."

The quiet, fast and almost invisible movements of the staff fascinated Sophie. They had no sooner finished tea when a maid arrived to clear the tray and Dalton announced a visitor.

"Mr. Sid Forester to see you see you, sir."

"Show him in please." Switching to Italian although Sophie understood English perfectly well, he said, *"Sophie, Papa' ha degli affari da fare."*

Sophie skipped out of the room, understanding her father and Mr. Forester were talking business. Mr. Forester stood in front of his boss with cap in hand. The stance appeared subservient but the twist of his mouth indicated something else. *He's not subservient, he's defiant*, Alberto thought, finding himself guarded against the duplicity.

"Mr. Forester, I am pleased to meet you at last and thank you

7

for coming. I was expecting the general manager, Mr. Young, to join us. I am anxious for news about the progress in the mill. When can we start operating?"

Mr. Forester shook Alberto's extended hand. "Mr. Young sent his apologies. He had a prior engagement."

"Please accept my apologies for our delay; my wife is not well and she needed to rest in London before continuing to Derby."

"It was perhaps a good thing that you were delayed. Although the mill is ready for operation, the silk arrived two days ago and we are only just ready to start. I thought you would prefer to be in attendance."

"Certainly. Are there any issues or problems? Do we have enough workers? I expect the men to work hard. I don't take kindly to laggards."

"We will have a better idea of any problems once we have had a trial run. The equipment is installed and ready. The workers are the best I can find."

"Mr. Forester, it is up to you as foreman to keep the workers motivated and disciplined. I strive to be a fair employer and expect good work in return. How many do you have working tomorrow?"

"Enough for a trial and to start the spinning but most are expected to start on Monday. As soon as we have enough thread, we'll start the looms and bring the weavers in. We already have orders."

"I'll discuss the orders with Mr. Young tomorrow. It's the operation and workers that are my immediate concern. Unless you have anything else to say, I will see you at the mill at eight tomorrow morning to start the trial."

Alberto poured himself another brandy and sat in a burgundy-coloured wingback leather chair. He looked at the glass and smiled. He'd only been in Derby a few hours and he was already acting like an Englishman. He mused over the extensive household staff. Did they need all these people? Perhaps, he thought, until Martina was on her feet. His brow creased with worry and, if he was honest, guilt. Martina had not travelled well. Her refusal to learn English should have told him she had no intention of staying. He had stubbornly ignored her sadness, telling himself she would adapt in time. He hoped Sophie would influence her mother. She had embraced the move and spoke fluent English.

Mr. Forester puzzled him. he couldn't explain why he felt such unease. Forester's refined manner and impeccable dress belied his position of foreman. Alberto shook his head, trying to dismiss Forester's shifty, deceitful eyes. He was tired and hungry.

The grandfather clock struck seven-thirty. He climbed the stairs, opened the bedroom door, and sat on the edge of the bed, watching Martina sleep. He worried that her breath sounded raspy and she looked flushed.

"*Martina, come stai?* Alberto said in Italian.

Martina rolled onto her back and gave him a weak smile, brushing the back of her hand against her brow.

There was a knock on the door and Bianca, the maid, entered with a tray of broth and toast. Martina screwed up her face and wafted the maid away, rolling over and closing her eyes. "*Andate e lasciatemi da sola.*"

"*Si Signora.*" Bianca frowned.

"Leave her to sleep." Alberto kissed Martina on the cheek. "I'll come back after I've had dinner with Sophie."

* * *

9

After breakfast the next morning, Sophie sat beside her and read Charles Dickens' *Little Dorrit*. Bianca had puffed up Martina's pillows and sat her up. Sophie thought she looked better and wanted to show her mother the house and garden.

"Mamma, oggi ti alzi? Desidero mostrarti la casa e il giardino."

Martina mopped her brow again. *"Forse domani."* Sophie could see beads of perspiration and wondered if that was normal. Mrs. Simpson entered and asked Sophie to ask her mother in Italian if she needed the doctor.

"Mamma, la Signora Simpson chiede se deve chiamare il medico?"

"No, grazie, sto bene. Non preoccuparti tesoro." Sophie stared at her mother, taking time to translate while deciding whether or not to ignore her mother.

"Call the doctor," she said.

Mrs. Simpson looked puzzled. "I thought your mother said 'no'? No is universal in any language."

Sophie let her head flop down. "I want Mama to get better and I think the doctor can help."

Mrs. Simpson patted Sophie on the head and smiled. "I know you are worried. Ask your father. He must make the decision."

Sophie watched her mother slide down the bed, her face had turned ashen, making her flushed cheeks bright and doll-like.

"Come, let your mother rest. It is a lovely day. You can go play in the garden."

She ran around the garden, freeing herself of the stuffy house. The fresh air felt good in her lungs. She ran and ran. The garden stretched for what seemed like forever. It was autumn, the Michaelmas daisies thick and bright purple, the chrysanthemums a rich gold. She skipped into the rose garden and found roses blooming. She walked to the bottom and watched the novelty of a river flowing beside a garden.

Across the River Derwent stood a large, imposing building, the Romano Silk Mill. She wondered what her father was doing and which window might be his office. The bank was slippery and she almost fell in the water. Her heart racing, she skipped back to the house. Feeling hungry, she wandered downstairs to the kitchen

"Hello, Miss Sophie. Are you hungry? What would you like?" Cook said.

Sophie looked around the warm, welcoming kitchen. A scullery maid not much older than Sophie gave her a funny look. She would really have liked some pasta but she didn't think this cook would know what that was.

Cook stared at her for a minute. "Italian?" she asked. Sophie nodded slowly.

"Minestrone soup?"

Sophie nodded again and said *"Zuppa."*

A large bowl of zuppa was placed on the table. Sophie ate large chunks of crusty bread and carefully spooned the hot pasta and vegetable soup. It looked the same, yet Sophie found the taste different from the Italian zuppa. But it filled her and she ran out to play in the garden again until dark. She heard the carriage pull up at the front of the house.

"Tell me what you did today," Alberto called.

"I played in the garden. Mother was sleeping. She said she would play with me tomorrow. Cook made me minestrone soup and I ate in the kitchen."

"Shall we dine together tonight? How is your mother?"

Sophie felt ashamed. She had not been to see her mother since the morning but she was delighted at the thought of having dinner with her father. She slipped her hand into his as they walked up the stairs. Before they reached the bedroom door, the sound of her mother moaning and then shouting tightened Sophie's chest. Entering the room, her eyes fixed on her mother tossing and turning in the bed. Alberto leapt to the bed and felt her mother's head. "She's burning up. Sophie go fetch Mrs. Simpson. Quickly."

Sophie ran down the stairs her heart pounding in her chest and a horrible hurt in her stomach. Her mother was very ill.

"*Signora Simpson, Signora Simpson, venite presto, mia madre sta morendo, ha la febbre molto alta!* Sophie yelled in Italian and repeated in English, "Fever! She's dying!"

Mrs. Simpson immediately called the doctor and sent Bianca upstairs with a bowl of cool water and a cloth to help bring the fever down.

* * *

Sophie and her father didn't eat dinner that night. Cook gave them some bread, cheese and wine, and cordial for Sophie, while they waited for the doctor in the drawing room. The tone of the doctor's voice scared her. It was sombre and his face was serious—a slight shake of his head and she knew he was saying there was little hope. She ran up the stairs to her room and cried with anger because she had not made Mrs. Simpson call the doctor in the morning; she'd known something was wrong and still she went to play in the garden. Dalton heard her sobbing. He tried to reassure her that she had done nothing wrong. When he could not console her, he sent for Mrs. Simpson, but Alberto was the only person who could calm her. He took her into her mother's room and they sat at her side, caring for the raging fever all night. Sophie eventually fell asleep on her father's lap.

She felt him shake her gently and opened her eyes. Daylight was filtering through the crack in the curtain lighting up her mother's face. She was still and pale, no longer flushed or agitated. Sophie breathed a sigh of relief—her mother had recovered. Why wasn't she moving? She turned to her father and saw tears trickle down his cheeks; she had never seen her father cry. He gently pulled Sophie closer and kissed the top of her head saying "She's gone, Sophie. She's in heaven now."

A House in Mourning

Sophie felt dark and sinister. Mrs. Simpson had insisted she wore black for the day of her mother's funeral, even though she was not allowed to attend the service. She felt claustrophobic; the windows were curtained and covered in black crepe. She wanted to rip off the clothes of death, scream into the silence that she could bear it no more. She ran to the drawing room window and flung the curtains open to see sunshine. But there was no sunshine, just rain and the funeral carriages plodding down the driveway. Her father walked through the door, grey with grief, escorted by his brother, Uncle Roberto.

Many strangers entered the house and spoke in hushed voices, helping themselves to a lavish table of wine and food. Sophie stood beside her father but he didn't see her. Tears rolled down her face. She wanted her father's comfort. Uncle Roberto took her hand and wiped her tears.

"Uncle, what will happen to us without Mama? Papa is so sad and it's all my fault."

"Oh no, child, it was not your fault. Your mama had been ill for some time and she caught a chill. Her frail body could not fight the fever. The doctor did everything he could." Sophie felt some comfort from her uncle's words, but she still wished she had sent for the doctor earlier.

Roberto and Sophie walked through the French doors into the garden. The rain had stopped and the sun was shining through grey clouds. He sat on a bench inside the garden gazebo and patted the seat for Sophie to sit beside him. "It's dry here. You asked me what would happen to you without Mama. Your papa will take care of you, but he is very sad at the moment and busy with the mill. As you know, you have no cousins. Your aunt and I were not blessed with children." He stopped, smiled and took a deep breath before adding, "Aunt Maria and I would like you to come back to Italy and live with us on the farm."

Sophie hated her aunt's fussy ways. She jumped up from the bench and ran into the house sobbing. "Papa, Papa, don't let them take me!"

Alberto looked at his daughter, shaken from his grief. "Whatever is the matter? Who's taking you?" Sophie's words could not be heard beyond her sobs. She couldn't stop and she couldn't breathe and started to choke. Alberto picked her up and carried her to her room.

"Papa, I want to stay with you."

"Sophie, of course you will stay with me. Please tell me what happened?" Sophie told him what her uncle had said, watching her father's face carefully. She saw shock and confusion.

"I think Uncle Roberto is being kind, but I promise I will not send you to Italy. Derby is our home. Your uncle means well." Alberto held his daughter until she relaxed. His thoughts wandered to his secret and the future he had planned for Sophie. He wished he had confided his plan to Martina. He couldn't help wondering if she would have approved of their daughter running a silk mill, or would she have expected Sophie to be a lady? He wanted her approval. His reluctance to share his secret told him he had not been sure of Martina's consent. Now he would never know for certain.

* * *

Alberto kept busy with the mill and recovered quickly from his wife's death. He ordered the black crepe to be removed and the mourning to cease, with many disapproving looks from the staff. Sophie had become morose, surrounded by so much black and silence, and he hated being reminded of his wife's death. Alberto didn't heed protocol and grieved in his own way.

Oak House no longer had a mistress. Alberto determined that he and Sophie did not need all the maids and reduced the house servants to Dalton, Cook, a gardener, Mrs. Simpson and one maid.

Mrs. Simpson tried to persuade Mr. Romano that Sophie needed a governess now that she did not have a mother. Her pleas went unheeded. Sophie began her education at Derby High School and with Mrs. Simpson's guidance she learned to take care of herself. The Romano Silk Mill opened two weeks later, after several successful trials. Immersed in the business, working tirelessly to produce and promote Romano silk, Alberto masked his grief and guilt. He missed Martina every day. Only Sophie and the mill kept him alive.

* * *

A year after the mill began production, the British aristocracy were clamouring for the Romano silk.

"Good morning!" Alberto called to the workers as he walked through the mill and up the stairs to his office. His voice was barely heard over the noise of the machines but the workers already expected his greeting and responded in unison. Mr. Forester shrugged and yelled, "Get back to work."

Alberto smiled, covering his concern that Sid Forester was a troublemaker, although he could not substantiate his suspicions. So far there had been no major labour issues. His instincts told him that Sid Forester was not who he claimed to be. His clothes were no longer crisp, but his speech indicated a background of privilege, not labour.

A little breathless from running up the stairs from the factory floor, Alberto extended his greeting: "It is a fine morning, Mr. Young, although I do find the English climate dull at this time of the year. But the clattering of the looms is music to my ears."

"The music of profit, Mr. Romano. We are close to capacity. I received a telephone call from Harrods this morning. They doubled their order of the white Angel Silk for the debutante season. Society mothers are taken with the name."

"Ah, I'm pleased. I hoped that naming the silks would prompt sales. The mothers associate the angel name with their daughters. I think of my own daughter as an angel."

"The strategy has definitely brought results. We also received an inquiry from Paris for samples." Mr. Young handed him the letter.

"I am surprised about Paris. The Lyon Silk Mill produces fine silk, which is not dissimilar to ours."

"It appears to be a special request from one of their customers."

Alberto pointed to the letter. "They plan to send their buyer next week." He stood at the glass window that overlooked the factory floor. Sid Forester's face was taut as he made a threatening gesture towards a young woman. The reason was not obvious.

"What do you know about Sid Forester?" Alberto asked, turning to face Mr. Young. "His attitude gives me cause for concern."

"He comes from a Macclesfield mill. No history of trouble, actually not much history at all. Would you like me to investigate further?"

"No."

"He works well and keeps production up. He's not very personable and has a bit of a chip on his shoulder."

"That chip is getting bigger and I find his bullying offensive. I am concerned about how he treats the workers, especially the women. Keep your eye on him and let me know if you suspect there's anything unusual."

Mr. Young hesitated for a few seconds and said. "We need Forester; he keeps production high. I can't say I like his attitude, but it works. I am more troubled about the silk supply. Mr. Romano, we need to speed up deliveries from Italy. With this last order from Harrods, the orders outnumber the bales of silk. If the next shipment doesn't arrive in the next couple of days, production will stop."

"Roberto doubled the shipment."

"I know but it hasn't arrived."

"I'll send a cable and find out when it left the farm."

The thought of stopping production was out of the question.

Roberto had promised the shipment two days ago. Alberto cabled his agent in London, where the shipment would dock, asking if it had arrived. He was relieved that the reply confirmed the shipment had arrived in London and was on the train, expected to arrive in Derby tomorrow. But this was cutting it far too close. Roberto was good at farming and silk throwing but, in spite of Alberto's tutelage, he had difficulty grasping the business. Did he need to take a trip to Lucca? His thoughts were broken by the office door opening and the racket of the factory burst in with Sid Forester.

"There's a rumour going round that we've run out of silk and you are stopping production."

"Where did you hear that?" Alberto yelled over the noise. "And close the door." Alberto looked puzzled. "The shipment is due tomorrow."

"Err…that is good news because we don't want the workers thinking of going on…" Sid's words trailed off.

"Thinking of what?"

"Nothing! Excuse me, I have schedules to set up."

"Mr. Forester, is there a problem?"

"No, sir."

Alberto glanced at Mr. Young after Forrester had left the office. "What was that all about? How did he know the shipment was late? He was taunting me, or threatening a work stoppage. Is he connected to any unions?"

"I don't think so, but the same thought crossed my mind. I certainly didn't tell him."

* * *

Alberto usually dined early so that he could eat with Sophie.

19

He glanced at his pocket watch, six-thirty. He needed to rush home. Today he looked forward to telling her about the Angel Silk order and the inquiry from Paris.

"Papa, you are late today. Cook made an Italian dinner for us tonight."

Alberto raised an eyebrow. "Italian. How thoughtful of her. Let us not keep her waiting." He took his daughter's arm and they settled at the dining room table.

Dalton arrived, carrying a large, steaming bowl, and began serving Cook's version of spaghetti Bolognese. Alberto stared at the fat limp spaghetti and thick lumps of tomato sauce piled on top. He smiled at Dalton. "Thank you. This looks delicious. Grated Parmesan cheese?"

Dalton looked puzzled. "Cheese? I'll ask Cook, sir."

Sophie could not contain herself any longer, and glancing towards her father she burst into giggles.

Trying his hardest to stifle his amusement, Alberto said, "Be gracious Sophie, Cook has tried hard and I am sure it will taste wonderful, if somewhat unusual. I suggest we find your mother's recipe and give it to her in a day or two."

Dalton returned with a dish of grated cheese. "Cook sends her apologies. She has run out of Parmesan cheese and hopes cheddar will substitute for today."

"It will suffice, and Dalton, thank her for the kind thought. This looks delicious, don't you agree Sophie?"

Sophie put her fork into the colourful mound, and nodded.

By the time the apple pie and custard arrived, Alberto had told her all about the new orders.

"Paris," she sighed. "Papa, Paris sounds so romantic. Can we go one day? Mama would have liked Paris. I miss her. I wanted to tell her about school when I came home today."

"I know, my angel. I miss her too. I would like to hear about school. Will I do?"

"Of course. I had top marks in arithmetic today. The teacher said girls are not usually good at mathematics but that I show promise. The other girls groan when we have an arithmetic test, but I like it. And English is fun. The teacher said that I must be smart because my mother tongue is Italian. What is mother tongue?"

"It is the language you were born with. Yours is Italian because you were born in Italy and your parents speak Italian."

"So if I was born in England my mother tongue would be English. You taught me English while we were in Italy but that doesn't count?"

"It means you speak two languages but Italian is your mother tongue. You are clever, my dear. I shall teach you how to run a business and when you are old enough you can take over the Romano Silk Mill."

"I would like that. When can I come and see the mill?"

"How about a visit during your school Christmas holidays?"

Mrs. Simpson knocked on the door. "Excuse me, sir, Sophie has some homework."

Sophie kissed her father and went to her room. She thought about running the silk mill and decided it would be exciting.

Monsieur Dubois

The cable sat prominently on Alberto's desk. He raised an eyebrow at such an early morning delivery, immediately concerned that something was amiss in Lucca. He ripped the envelope open and the name Dubois jumped off the page. He went down to the factory floor, yelling over the machines: "Monsieur Dubois from Paris is arriving at two this afternoon. Please make sure everything is running well."

"Yes, sir." Mr. Forester's smile and his compliance surprised Alberto.

He ran up the stairs to his office and called the house to ask Mrs. Simpson to make up a guest room and inform Cook to expect a guest for dinner; a business meeting.

Hands clasped behind his back, Alberto walked over to the outside window and stared down at the enormous wheel as it harnessed the power of the river to turn the gears that operated the looms. Such noisy, clumsy machines, he mused, a contrast to the delicate silk they produced. The thought heightened

22

his feelings of ambiguity about the Frenchman's visit. His acute business sense was being challenged and he didn't trust Monsieur Dubois. The last thing he needed was his designs and secrets turning up in Paris. The enticing names of Romano's superior silk had reached ears at some French fashion houses. No orders yet, but it was only a matter of time.

* * *

Monsieur Dubois spoke excellent English, much to Alberto's relief, as his French was adequate at best. The meeting began in the office. Alberto proudly spread the silk samples in a semicircle on his desk, the only one missing was the Angel Silk, which he had no intention of sharing.

"Beautiful." Monsieur Dubois sighed and admiration spread across his face as he felt the smooth fabric. "The weaving is magnificent and the colours vibrant. The Lyon mill cannot match this quality. How do you produce such fine fabric?"

Alberto nodded, acknowledging the compliment, and smiled. "We have our secrets, sir." Alberto reluctantly led the Frenchman out of his office onto the factory floor, where Forester appeared uninvited. The Frenchman was bombarding Alberto with questions about the spinning and weaving process. Dissatisfied with Alberto's vague answers, he directed his questions to Forester.

"Monsieur Dubois, Mr. Forester's knowledge of processes are limited to his duties as foreman." Alberto was thankful that his shrewd business mind had sensed Forester's duplicity and prevented him from disclosing the Romano secrets. Frustrated, Alberto continued, "May I ask why you are so persistent regarding our spinning process?"

"You spin a fine silk and if I am to buy some, I would like to know more about it."

"Forgive me, I am sure you will agree that it is the quality of the finished product that is important to you. I don't believe knowing the process is of any value." Alberto gave a short laugh, his face serious; he stared directly at his guest. "Unless of course you are more interested in the Romano spinning and weaving techniques."

Silence.

"My interest is as one silk-man to another."

"Then you will understand when I say that the quality of the fabric is primarily due to the quality of the raw silk. The Romano silkworms produce an unusually fine thread. But Lyon produces an excellent silk. Monsieur Dubois, has someone specifically requested Romano Silk?" Alberto was becoming more suspicious and concerned that one or more of the French fashion houses had approached Dubois.

Monsieur Dubois gave a nod, said nothing, and glanced at Forester. The brief connection did not escape Alberto and he was beginning to think that even a limited tour of the mill was a mistake. Especially when Monsieur Dubois lingered over the loom weaving the cobalt blue fabric and he exclaimed, "It is exquisite."

Alberto caught his elbow and moved him away from the loom. "The tour is over. Please wait in the lobby."

It was obvious that the Frenchman greatly admired the silk, but equally obvious he was not going to place an order. Perhaps over dinner later, Alberto thought. He ran upstairs to his office and ordered the carriage. Descending the stairs, he heard voices speaking fluent French. The animated conversation was between Sid Forester and a red-faced Monsieur Dubois.

24

He pulled back into the shadows and tried to listen but the noise from the mill drowned their words. Taking a deep breath, he casually walked down the stairs. "Mr. Forester, don't you have work to do? Monsieur Dubois, the carriage is waiting. Shall we?"

The journey to the house was longer than it appeared. Oak House sat across the River Derwent from the mill but the only bridge was a mile down the road.

Dalton showed the gentlemen into the study and began pouring sherry. "Miss Sophie would like to see you, sir."

"Please ask her to come in." Alberto sat by the fire and invited Monsieur Dubois to sit in the opposite chair. "My daughter is anxious to meet a gentleman from Paris. Would you indulge her for a few minutes? We can discuss business over dinner." Sophie came bounding through the door. Alberto was taken aback, she looked so much like her mother. Her long ebony hair curled and hung gracefully on her shoulders and her brown eyes sparkled with excitement. She wore a pale blue dress that Alberto thought might be too grown up for his little girl.

"Monsieur Dubois, allow me to introduce my daughter, Sophie." Sophie stretched her arm, quickly glancing at her father.

"*S'il vice plait de vice reencounter*". Sophie grinned; she had been practicing all day.

Monsieur Dubois stood up and bent forward kissing Sophie's hand. "It is my pleasure, *Mademoiselle Sophie.*"

"Come sit with us." Alberto indicated a chair next to him. "Dalton, would you fetch Miss Sophie some cordial please?"

"Monsieur, Papa tells me you live in Paris. Please tell me about Paris. Is it as beautiful and romantic as people say? Is there music in the streets?"

25

"Sophie, not too many questions," her father warned.

"It's a big, dirty city. The River Seine flows through the middle, like the River Derwent flows through Derby. It is an artist's town, many painters and writers come to Paris. Most are poor and beg for money with cheap art instead of working. A nuisance, giving Paris an image of romance; a poor excuse for laziness. I'm a businessman and have no time for such frivolous things. Romance, what is that?" He wafted his hand, dismissing Sophie. Her eyes moistened but she quickly recovered. "Mama was an artist and she saw beauty in everything. She told me many times that without beauty, there is no soul."

Monsieur Dubois shifted in his chair and sipped his sherry. "Well, artists don't make money and most of the artists in Paris are starving. I don't see the beauty in poverty and souls are the church's responsibility." He laughed and settled back in his chair, proud of his wit. He directed his next comment to Alberto. "My interest is in the aristocratic society of Europe—and their money. It is my intention to be the largest silk producer in all of Europe. Starving artists don't buy silk to fill my coffers with francs. Don't you agree Mr. Romano?"

Sophie looked at her father. Already disappointed, she was afraid of what he might say. "Monsieur Dubois, I hold in high esteem the opinions of my late wife and my daughter. I appreciate beauty and artists. I consider our profession to be a form of art: The art of the silkworms spinning their cocoons, the art of silk throwing, the tender care of such delicate thread and finally creating patterns to weave into beautiful fabrics, which you yourself admired this afternoon. There is as much value in the beauty as there is in the money; I don't think it is possible to have one without the other."

Monsieur Dubois made a *cuffuf* noise and Sophie stifled a

giggle, relieved when Dalton announced dinner was served. She kissed her father and whispered, "I don't like that man. He's not to be trusted, Papa. He has no soul."

Alberto smiled, loving his daughter more than he thought possible. "Good night, sweet Sophie."

Sophie hesitated, wanting to ignore the visitor; she glanced at her father and saw his disapproval. She grinned, making her point by waiting until she opened the study door, "Good night, monsieur."

The dinner of roast beef was magnificent. Alberto had delicately suggested an English meal, not wanting Cook to try her hand again at an Italian dish. He had selected a robust cabernet to complement the beef, and regretted wasting such a good wine on the Frenchman. Neither man had achieved his goal. Alberto had no silk order from Paris and Monsieur Dubois had found no secrets. After dinner, Dubois excused himself, refusing Alberto's offer of a bed. He had reservations at the Railway Hotel.

Tired, uneasy and disappointed, Alberto retired to his study with a glass of brandy. He missed Martina and wished he could ask her opinion. He smiled, remembering Sophie's cleverness and recognized that she was her mother's daughter. Her words came back to him, "He's not to be trusted. He has no soul." At the same time, he recalled the Frenchman's words, "I intend to be the largest and best silk producer in all of Europe." The Frenchman was giving him a message. Was it a warning or a challenge?

* * *

Disheartened with the outcome of the previous day's events,

Alberto arrived at the mill early the next morning. Calling his usual good morning to the workers as he walked across the mill floor, he indicated to Forester to join him in the office.

"Mr. Forester, I couldn't help but notice you were speaking fluent French with our guest yesterday. When did you learn French?"

"My grandmother was born in Lyon in France. She taught me when I was young. Why? Is speaking French a crime?"

"No, of course not. I am concerned because the conversation appeared less than pleasant. Why would Monsieur Dubois be angry with you?"

"I was not aware that he was angry. We spoke only of the silk spinning." The polite words, yet again, were edged with defiance.

"Yes, indeed," Alberto added, "He seemed overly interested in our spinning process."

Forester smiled and leaned forward congenially. His deliberate change in posture did not escape Alberto. "The Romano silk is finer than the Lyon silk and yet our process is the same. Why is that?"

"Is that what he was asking you yesterday?" Alberto shook his head. "The Romano raw silk is finer than most, resulting in a finer fabric. The Romano secret is the care and attention we give our silk and some methods we use in the weaving process."

Forester took a breath to reply but changed his mind. Alberto thought he looked troubled and wondered if he was being coerced by the Frenchman; or was his interest for personal gain? Either way, he was not to be trusted.

"Forester, you are an excellent foreman, a little harsh on the workers at times, but you get the job done. Production and quality increases every day because of your tenacity. I am an honest businessman and believe in treating my workers fairly. In return I expect loyalty and hard work. You are a hard worker, with that I have no issues. But loyalty…I have my doubts. Disloyalty has no place in the Romano Mill."

Sid Forester stood up, his face tight with anger, his fiery words spit into Alberto's face, "I take offense at such accusations."

"If I offend, I apologize. I expect you to alleviate my doubts, Mr. Forester. You are a valued employee and I would like to keep it that way." Alberto fixed his gaze, waiting for his reply.

"Sir, I do believe Monsieur Dubois' visit was to elicit secrets. He realized during the tour of the mill that I was fluent in French. The confrontation you overheard at the front entrance was, as you deduced, somewhat heated. He was accusing me of being aware of the Romano secrets. I told him I knew of no secrets. The Frenchman tried to bribe me. First with a position in the Lyon Mill and, when I refused, he offered me a considerable amount of money, which I also refused. He discovered no secrets, but he is angry and jealous over the Romano Mill's success and I fear he will try to discredit us. It will not be my doing. I think that attests to my loyalty, sir."

"Indeed it does and I appreciate your candor. Your loyalty will be rewarded. I hope we never hear from Monsieur Dubois again."

Comfortable with Sid Forester's explanation but somewhat dubious that he had heard the last of Dubois, Alberto joined Mr. Young to try and resolve the problem of the delayed orders from Lucca.

The Letter

❧

H is pen poised over a sheet of linen writing paper, Alberto couldn't form the words. His gaze fixed on Sophie, who was attempting to make a snowman with a thin layer of January snow. *She's growing up*, he thought, *one minute she acts as a young lady and another she's a child at play*. Hearing Dalton enter his study, he turned. "I'll stoke the fire, sir. Miss Sophie will be cold when she comes in."

"Thank you. Please ask Cook for hot cocoa instead of tea this afternoon, and some hot buttered crumpets." Alberto enjoyed Sundays at home. He would normally be spending time with Sophie but he needed to write his brother a letter. It was harder than he thought:

Dear Roberto,

I hope you and Maria are well and all is well at the farm. Business in Derby is excellent. The Romano silk has quite a reputation. Orders increase every day; Harrods, our best customer, has a clientele of society ladies who like our silk.

I have been summoned to London to speak with the buyer at Henry Poole & Co of Savile Row. They are bespoke tailors serving the British elite and royalty, including King Edward. I said I would put us on the map, dear brother, and that is happening as I write.

However, my reason for writing is of a more serious nature...

Alberto stopped.

"Papa, what is wrong?" Sophie skipped into the study with Dalton at her heels. "Yum, crumpets and cocoa."

"I'm writing a difficult letter to Uncle Roberto."

"Is it about the silk from Lucca?"

"Yes." Taken aback by Sophie's correct supposition, Alberto frowned. "How did you know?"

"I heard you talking to Mr. Young when I was at the mill."

"It's bad manners to eavesdrop." Alberto's smile belied the reprimand. "But you are right, I am concerned about the slow deliveries from Lucca."

"Papa, Uncle Roberto doesn't have a head for business. I've heard you say that a million times. You must send him instruction. Can you arrange the shipments from here and just tell him when it will be picked up?"

"I'm speechless. I had not thought of that. I have to manage what I can from here. Sophie, you are older than your years." Sophie beamed with pride at her father's approval.

"I'll help you write the letter."

Smiling, Alberto went to his desk and read what he had written. "The matter is serious and Roberto needs to understand that." He read aloud as he continued writing:

The delay in the shipments of silk from Lucca is causing a delay in the manufacture of the fabric, uncertainty in the workers at the mill, and dissatisfaction among our clients who have guaranteed delivery to their customers. The British upper class are not forgiving and are quite fickle. Can you imagine the King of England tolerating a delay?

If we cannot fill the orders on time, even the high quality of Romano silk will not be enough to keep our customers. They will seek better service elsewhere. The orders are coming in so fast at the moment that I think it would be more efficient for Derby to determine quantities and arrange shipping dates. I will speak with Mr. Young tomorrow, today being Sunday, to make arrangements with the shipper. You will be notified of the shipping dates in advance. All you need to do is have the silk ready for pickup on the specified dates.

Sophie giggled. "Is the King of England wearing Romano silk? How romantic, Papa." Sophie nodded her approval. Satisfied with the letter, Alberto joined her by the warm fire and the two ate crumpets and drank cocoa.

* * *

St. Pancras train station reminded Alberto of an ant colony;

everyone scurrying from one place to the next. He hailed a cab and gave the driver the address for Henry Poole & Co on Savile Row. The cabbie looked him up and down, repeating the address and giving Alberto the distinct impression that his attire did not match the destination. Until now, he had not given much thought to his tailor, but perhaps the Derby tailor was not good enough. Now that the business was moving in different circles, a Henry Poole suit might be more appropriate. He liked that idea. In fact, he thought a Henry Poole suit would separate Alberto Romano from his competitors.

The cab stopped. "This the right place?"

"Yes, thank you."

Patting his leather case that held a selection of Romano silk samples, Alberto took a deep breath and pushed open the heavy glass door of the shop. An older, grey-haired gentleman approached him. "Good afternoon, sir." Alberto felt the gentleman's eyes scan his clothing and his pursed lips tightened but his expression did not alter. "May I help you?" Alberto wondered at how the British showed disdain without moving a muscle. He definitely needed a Henry Poole suit. But first he must secure the order.

"Good morning! My name is Alberto Romano of Romano Silk. I have an appointment with Mr. Grantham."

The gentleman softened a little. "Please take a seat and I'll see if Mr. Grantham is available."

The pomp of the British aristocracy permeated the store. A large, rounded mirror stood above an ornate wooden mantel where a clock chimed two. An octagonal Victorian glass display case, supported by thick wooden spindles, stood in the centre of the store, harbouring a selection of gold and diamond cufflinks. A young man leaned against a corner counter and sewed intricate gold braid onto a red and gold jacket; livery for some palace or other, Alberto thought. He found himself holding his breath, afraid the noise of his breathing would interfere with decorum.

"Please come this way." Alberto followed the gentleman through a large room lined with high cutting tables, which the tailors used as benches. Sitting on top of the tables were twenty or more tailors, with a variety of partially sewn jackets draped across their laps as they rhythmically punched needles into collars and lapels, carefully pulling thread with great precision. No one spoke, the concentration intense as nimble fingers deliberately sewed each stitch. He was shown into a messy office strewn with fabric and haberdashery samples. The room consisted of a desk and two chairs, and a cabinet totally engulfed in fabric. Alberto couldn't help but notice the contrast from the neat storefront.

"Mr. Romano, the reputation of the Romano silk has become quite the chatter in the tailoring and dressmaking circles of London. I understand you supply fabric to Harrods for ladies' attire."

"Yes, we do. The fine white silk called Angel Silk is particularly suitable for young debutantes. I have other silks and designs suitable for gentleman's attire."

"I am actually interested in one particular silk. Your reputation has reached the ears of His Majesty King Edward." Alberto gulped. He had thought his grandiose speculation expressed to Sophie and Roberto was more fantasy than likely to come true.

"What is it we can do for the King?"

"Several years ago the King, then the Prince of Wales, asked us to make him something like a smoking jacket, not as formal as tails; suitable for casual dining at Sandringham." He suppressed

34

a chuckle. "We cut off the tails and made him what is now known as the dinner jacket. The style we originally made for the Prince was made of silk—blue silk to be precise. The King has adopted this comfortable casual dinner jacket for entertaining his personal friends."

Alberto opened his leather bag and laid several samples of fabric on the desk. Mr. Grantham rubbed his chin and stared at the silk.

"The colours are magnificent." He fondled the fabric. "Mr. Romano, many different fabrics are presented to me. This silk is…the only word is exquisite." He picked up a rich deep blue and a watermarked deep red the colour of burgundy wine. "I know His Majesty's taste, and these two are perfect." Mr. Grantham pulled out a large order book, running his finger down the page as he checked and commented, matching silks to specific clients, and adding the material to the order. Alberto filled his notebook with Mr. Grantham's comments about client's preferences. Mr. Grantham scribbled quantities and styles in his order book and handed Alberto the official Henry Poole order. The mantel clock in the store struck four as he bid the gentleman goodbye.

He hailed a cab, directing the driver to Harrods in Knights-bridge. The meeting at Henry Poole's had taken longer than expected and he was late for this appointment. He smiled. Surely when the buyer discovered the delay was due to the King he would be forgiven. He jumped out of the cab and the green-coated doorman directed him to the administration office. A sour looking secretary frowned at him. "You are thirty-five minutes late," adding, "Sir," as an afterthought, making obvious her disapproval of such bad manners.

"My sincere apologies, I was detained at Henry Poole's &

Co." Staring directly at her, he grinned. "Finalizing details of an order for His Majesty King Edward. Please notify Mr. Sinclair."

"Please take a seat." The humbled secretary disappeared behind a large oak door, reappearing almost immediately and holding the door open she said, "Mr. Sinclair will see you now."

Alberto's visit to Harrods was a courtesy call rather than to secure orders. Mr. Sinclair placed most of his orders by post or telephone. However, Alberto was delighted when his short visit precipitated an increase in Harrods' existing orders. In the space of ten minutes, Alberto was on his way back to St. Pancras for the evening train.

The day's events had given him an appetite. He went straight to the dining car for an early dinner. Sipping a sherry, he opened his notebook and unfolded the official order from Henry Poole & Co., satisfied that the Romanos had reached the pinnacle of success.

* * *

Happy and tired, Alberto was greeted by Dalton at the front door of Oak House. He ran up the stairs and crept into Sophie's bedroom, intending to tell her all about the London visit. He stood at the end of her bed and watched her sleep. Deciding the news could wait until morning, he left her to her dreams and made his way to his own room.

Alberto slept well knowing his visit to London had sealed the success of Romano Silk. Anxious to tell Sophie the good news, Alberto dressed hurriedly. He tapped on her door but, receiving no answer, he ran down the stairs to find her already at the breakfast table.

"Good morning, Sophie. Today is a spectacular day. I have some very exciting news." Alberto related his trip to London in great detail.

"Papa, this wonderful news." Sophie stood up and danced around the breakfast table, much to Dalton's annoyance as a tray of toast fell on the floor.

"Papa, I will be the envy of Derby High School when I tell the girls the King of England wears Romano silk. Will you meet the King? Perhaps we'll be invited to Buckingham Palace. I'll be a debutante dressed in the Romano Angel Silk."

"Slow down, Sophie. We are supplying Henry Poole & Co. with silk. It is the tailors who make the jackets for the King. I will not see the King, nor will we be invited to the Palace, and I'm sorry but no debutante ball for you." Sophie plunked herself in a chair and pouted.

Alberto laughed, softly amused by the child inside the young lady. "Pouting is not becoming of a young lady. Don't be disappointed. The prestige of being known to supply Harrods and Savile Row is enormous. We have made our mark on business and society."

Sophie brightened and picked up her satchel for school and the two left the house together, both eager to announce the news of royal connections.

"Good morning!" Alberto called entering the factory floor. He beckoned to Mr. Young to come down from the office and called Forester and the workers to slow the machines and gather round to hear the good news. The workers let out an enormous cheer, the women at the looms giggled and Mr. Young beamed. Only Sid Forester seemed less than happy with the news. Alberto called a meeting with Mr. Young and Forester to plan the scheduling to accommodate the new orders.

Alberto directed his concern to Forester. "You do not seem happy about the news."

"Of course, it is great news, but we are already operating at capacity." Forester said and Mr. Young nodded in agreement.

"I am aware of that. We need to start an evening shift."

Forester gave a long sigh of exasperation. "Mr. Romano, we don't have enough skilled workers for the day shift. I can't man an extra shift."

"Hire all the workers you need. Source some skilled workers from Macclesfield—you used to work there. Now get started." Forester shook his head as he left the office.

* * *

Two weeks later Alberto shouted "Good evening!" to the new evening shift as he walked out of the mill to join Sophie for dinner.

"Have a good evening, Mr. Romano," said Davies, the new night foreman. Alberto didn't know him well but he found his attitude refreshing and polite in contrast to Forester's surly, even secretive attitude. He hadn't been a troublemaker and he could not find fault with his work, but Alberto could not trust him.

Dalton handed him a letter from Italy as he walked through the door. Anxious to read Roberto's letter he went into the study and ripped the envelope.

Dear Alberto,
It is good to hear from you and to know you and

Sophie are in good health. We are all well in Lucca and the farm is thriving. What wonderful news about your success. Orders for King Edward, that is a remarkable accomplishment, brother. I hope I can do as well here and produce enough silk.

I agree that it is more efficient for you to arrange shipping and I am relieved not to have to worry. I am concerned about the quantities, remember we are limited to the worms' cycle and storage for the low cycle.

Alberto looked up as Sophie came into the study. "A letter from your uncle."

"Does he like our idea?"

"Yes, you were right Sophie; your uncle is happy to pass on the responsibility. I am pleased that is settled."

Italy 1911 – Silk Farm Troubles

After three years of success, the Romano silk was a household name in the best houses in England. Only Alberto was aware of the struggle to maintain a consistent flow of raw material from Lucca. The constant telephone calls and letters required to manage the farm business and correct Roberto's mistakes weren't enough. The business teetered on the edge of a cliff and Alberto hung on by his finger tips. The last silk shipment was not only late, but short by several bales. The raw silk would be gone by the end of the summer. His biggest concern a slight deterioration in the quality. There was no alternative; the farm needed Alberto's attention. A trip to Italy was essential.

* * *

Roberto waved frantically at the train as it pulled into Lucca station. The brothers hugged and laughed and slapped each other on the back.

"My goodness, little Sophie has grown up." Roberto kissed his niece, and turning to his brother he said, "She's beautiful, just like Martina. We'll have to watch the lustful Italian boys or find her a suitable husband."

"Not yet. Let her be a child for a little while longer." Alberto said, squeezing Sophie's shoulders.

"I'm not a child, Papa. I am sixteen and an adult."

"I am very proud of my little girl. She graduated with the highest marks in the whole school and already has a head for business. When she finishes secretarial school she will join me in the mill. This summer, I would like you to teach her all you know about cultivating silkworms."

"It would be my pleasure to teach the next generation of Romanos my passion." He smiled at Sophie. "Do you think you are up to the task?" Roberto turned away before Sophie could answer and loaded the luggage into the truck.

"How are things at the farm?" Alberto asked, taking off his jacket and hoping for some relief from the scorching Italian summer heat. Roberto shrugged, avoiding his brother's eyes he stared at the road. "Your anxiety shows brother. Was it a good decision for me to come?"

"It was. Things are difficult at the farm."

Alberto felt his heart drop. His concerns about the farm were valid.

"I think we'll have to cut labour costs."

"Why? The sale of silk to England and Bologna should be enough to operate the farm and make a profit. What has happened?" The pit of his stomach clenched as he braced himself for what he would find at the farm.

Sophie gasped as they approached the farm entrance. She remembered the majestic, ornate black wrought-iron gates

41

that heralded the entrance to the esteemed Romano Silk Farm. She blinked, hoping that when her eyes opened her childhood memories would be real. Instead the gates stood open, the wrought iron dripping rust along the intricate swirls. The truck bounced from one hole to the next along the dirt road, totally depleted of gravel. Roberto glanced at his brother. "Sorry about the bumpy ride. It was a rainy spring and with more trucks going too and fro, it's hard to keep up."

The sight at the end of the road was no better. The villa that Alberto, Martina and Sophie had called home was overgrown with plants and weeds and peeling paint on the dark blue shutters made them look mottled. She visualized her last memory of the neat garden full of flowers her mother tended so lovingly and her mother crying quietly as her father closed the door for the last time. She wondered if her childhood memories had glorified the silk farm, but her father's expression confirmed that her recollections were accurate.

Uncle Roberto pulled up to the farmhouse and Aunt Maria greeted them at the once-red door, now sun bleached to a washed-out pink. Red and yellow hibiscus bloomed in the front, and an enormous pomegranate bush, ten feet tall and ten feet wide, took over most of the parched lawn. Aunt Maria kissed, stroked and patted Sophie as if she were a pet dog. Sophie hated her aunt's fussing and passed quickly. Inside, the house was neat, clean and cool; the shutters still closed against the afternoon heat. The kitchen table had glasses, wine and trays of bread, meat and cheese laid out. At the sight of food Sophie realized she was hungry.

"I didn't open up the villa, I thought you could stay at the house. Maria thought it best as Sophie will be staying for the summer after you return to England." Roberto looked to his brother for approval.

"Of course. I'll visit the villa later."

* * *

Sophie came downstairs quietly before Aunt Maria fussed over breakfast, finding Alberto making coffee.

"Good morning, Father."

Alberto smiled. "Good morning, Sophie. Why so formal this morning?"

"I think Papa is too childish now. I am sixteen and will soon be working at the mill. I would prefer to call you Father."

"Father is fine. Would you like espresso or caffélatte?"

"Caffélatte, Pa..I mean, Father."

"I plan to take a walk around the farm this morning. Will you join me?"

"Yes. Will Uncle Roberto show us around?"

"Perhaps. He is already working. We'll catch up with him as soon as we've had coffee and cornettos." Seeing Sophie's puzzled look Alberto added, "Breakfast pastries. Don't you remember how your mother used to make them? I think Aunt Maria makes them from the same recipe. I found these in the pantry, left over from yesterday."

Taking a bite of the traditional pastry Sophie replied, "Um, I do remember, they are good."

* * *

Father and daughter walked around the farm, through the mulberry trees and into the silk shed. Much to Alberto's delight Sophie, was fascinated with the process and asked question after question.

"Father, what is it? You frown."

"The farm is in disarray. The trees are not being pruned properly. The buildings are in need of repair. I don't see any workers. Something is wrong."

Sophie grabbed her father's hand. "What shall we do?"

"First we'll breakfast and then I'll talk with Uncle Roberto. Nothing to worry about, I'm sure."

After breakfast, anxious to escape her aunt's fussing, Sophie took a book and settled on a little bench under an olive tree. She sighed with satisfaction; the tranquility suited her as childhood memories flooded back. Memories of her mother almost sparked tears. Unexpectedly, she felt sad, not just for the absence of her mother but for everything around her. Her father's words 'something is wrong' stuck in her mind. Something *was* wrong.

She placed her book on the bench, unable to concentrate. She wandered over to the villa and turned the door handle. The door creaked as it opened. A musty smell hit her nostrils, the silence so deep she could hear it in her ears. Carefully placing her feet on the once-polished wood, she gently closed the door as though someone was sleeping. Walking on tip-toe she went into the kitchen, her mother stood by the stove, she turned and smiled.

"Mama!" Sophie called but the vision had gone. She walked to her old bedroom, leaving footprints on the dusty floor. She had a warm feeling seeing two sets of footprints—she was happy her mother had come home. Her favourite doll sat on the bed, picking her up she remembered deciding she was too grown up to take her to England and then regretting her decision when she missed her. The front door creaked open and her heart flipped, for a split second she thought it was her mother but her father called, "Sophie, are you here?"

"Yes, Papa, I'm here."

"Nothing has changed; I can feel your mother. She loved it here and didn't want to move to England."

"I know, she came back. She's here, Papa."

Alberto put his arm around Sophie's shoulders. "I'm happy she's back but I'm sorry I took her to England. I think that is what killed her." He blinked back tears.

"Papa, you can't blame yourself."

"Perhaps not, but I miss her. She always listened to my worries and I could do with her ear right now. I'm being remorseful. I came to find you. Aunt Maria has prepared lunch."

"Why don't you sit here and tell Mama your worries, I think she's still listening."

He smiled at his daughter's wisdom and closed the front door. "I think I will come over later this evening. You are too wise, my dear Sophie."

Sophie went to bed early, after helping her aunt with the kitchen chores. Her father and uncle were sequestered in the office, talking business. She fell asleep and was woken by a loud argument. Her father's angry voice reached a pitch she had never heard before. "Why? Why? Roberto, you have squandered all our money…" A door slammed and she jumped out of bed and watched her father walk over to the villa.

She held her breath, trying to rid herself of a deep sense of dread. Uncle Roberto had been grumpy and bad tempered all through dinner. Aunt Maria had brushed away tears from a nasty remark. The kind uncle she had known as a child had changed. She heard Roberto's heavy feet thump up the stairs and Aunt Maria was crying again.

* * *

During the next two weeks, it seemed the argument was forgotten as the brothers worked together. Alberto paid off the considerable farm debt. Together they hired skilled sericulture workers; re-vamped schedules and processes. Maria, who was in charge of the books, was taught with Sophie how to keep the books up to date. Alberto tried to explain the signs that might indicate the business was not doing well.

Alberto took to spending time at the villa, where he found comfort feeling Martina's presence. He wondered whether it was Martina he sensed, or just a willingness to believe. Sophie certainly believed her mother haunted the villa, if that was the right term. Martina would never haunt anything, he thought. Sitting at the kitchen table he made the decision to go to Bologna even though Roberto insisted it wasn't necessary. His thoughts were interrupted as the front door creaked. Sophie called, "Father, are you here?"

"In the kitchen." Alberto waited for Sophie. "I have decided to take a trip to Bologna tomorrow. Would you like to join me?"

"Of course."

They left the farm before daylight the next morning, leaving a note for Roberto and Maria.

The Bologna Silk Mill, like the mill in Derby, dated back to the 17th century. The entrance lobby had a richness to it with drapes of colourful silk on the walls and decorative Italian pottery complementing the silks. A pretty signorina sat at a desk and greeted them with pleasantries.

Alberto introduced himself and asked to meet with Signor Matteo. The clatter of machinery escaped into the lobby as the heavy wooden door opened, leading into the factory. "Signor Matteo," she yelled over the noise and returned to her desk leaving the door open. Signor Matteo appeared closing the door and noise behind him.

"Alberto, what a surprise. What brings you to Bologna?"

"Franco, I would like to introduce my daughter Sophie. We are visiting my brother in Lucca. Sophie is learning sericulture. It would have been impolite not to call on our oldest and best customer. I apologize for not making an appointment but I am returning to England the day after tomorrow. Is it convenient or would you prefer we come back later this afternoon?"

Franco guided them to a pleasant conversation area in the lobby. "Please take a seat. Can I offer you refreshments? I have a few minutes before I must attend a meeting."

Sophie sat on the sofa, wondering why her father looked so worried as he took a seat opposite Franco.

"How is business in England?" Franco asked.

"Excellent. The mill is operating at close to capacity. The British gentry, including King Edward, have exquisite taste in fashion, which demands high quality silk. It is a challenge to keep up with the demand at times. And Bologna?"

"I'm impressed. Do you have a royal warrant?"

"No, but Henry Poole & Co of Savile Row do have the royal warrant. We supply the silk and they do the tailoring."

"Business is excellent here too. However, of late, your brother has difficulty meeting our orders."

"Oh? The farm is producing enough for both of us."

"There are times when Roberto cannot fill my orders and I'm afraid the quality of the silk has deteriorated. It is imperative

47

the quality of the raw silk be exact for our fine veil fabric. I'm sorry to say the last batch prompted me to search for other suppliers."

"I'm sorry to hear this. My brother said nothing of your dissatisfaction. I admit there have been problems at the farm. Roberto has no head for business so I am taking over some of the tasks and, during my visit, changes have been made. The silk is back to the quality you are accustomed to."

"I'm sorry, Alberto. I am meeting with the buyer of the Lyon Silk Mill this afternoon."

"Would his name be Monsieur Dubois?"

"Yes. Are you acquainted?"

"He visited the mill in Derby on the pretence of purchasing silk from us. After he accepted my hospitality and threatened a member of my staff, I realized his intentions were less than honourable. His intention was to steal the secret to the Romano silk. I would imagine he is looking for the secret to your veil fabric. Monsieur Dubois made it quite clear he intends to be the largest producer of fine silk in all of Europe."

"I didn't question his intention. He asked for a tour of the mill before he supplied us with raw silk."

"He asked me for a tour of the Derby mill. That must be his strategy. He had no intention of placing any orders. I believe his intent here is to put me out of business by supplying you with Lyon silk and then stealing your secrets and ultimately putting you out of business as well."

"I did think it an odd request. He told me the Romano Silk Farm had fallen into disarray and with the recent shortages and questionable quality, it was easy to believe." Franco shook his head. "His brother works in a silk mill in England and he implied that business was so bad they had switched to Lyon

48

Silk. He didn't name the mill but insinuated it was your Derby mill."

"The farm may have had issues but the mill is thriving—we are working at full capacity. I added an evening shift to accommodate the orders. It is not the Derby mill. Monsieur Dubois is lying. He saw the Derby Mill in full production. As far as I am aware, he has no association with the Romano farm. His comments are a lucky guess."

"He is a slippery character and very convincing."

"Franco, I can assure you that I have resolved the issues at the farm. The quality is back and supply is plentiful. On my return to England, I intend to hire a quality manager. I already have someone in mind."

"I have always trusted you, Alberto, and I would like to continue doing business with you. I need a guarantee."

"You have my guarantee. Please contact me anytime."

* * *

After a long meeting with Roberto, Alberto went to the villa and met Sophie. This was their safe haven, a place where they could remember Martina.

"Sophie, I have taught you what I can about the business here in Lucca. I want you to learn as much as you can from your uncle and aunt. I was never the farmer. Your uncle had a natural sense for sericulture, for me it was business. It was a mistake to give Roberto the responsibility of the farm business. I plan to do more. But for now, we have uncovered and resolved the issues with Signor Matteo. The debts are paid and the farm is in good shape. I can't find anything else that needs my attention." Alberto hesitated. "And yet I think your uncle is hiding something."

"I know, Papa."

"I don't want you to worry, and you are very young for me to ask this."

Sophie gave a little pout. "Father I am more grown up than you think."

"You are, my dear, and that is why I am asking you to monitor carefully. The farm is running well and Aunt Maria is up to date with the bookkeeping. It is important she keep up with invoices and payments. It is bad business to humour delinquent customers or overspend on supplies. Good workers must be paid well. Do you understand bookkeeping well enough to see mistakes?"

"I do. I know more than Aunt Maria."

"Tomorrow I leave for England. When you return at the end of the summer you can work with me in the mill. But first you must finish secretarial school."

"As you wish, Father."

Strangers and Strange Happenings

S ophie missed her father. Since her mother's death, they had never been apart. The quiet dinner table reflected her mood. Uncle Roberto hardly said a word. She realized how close the brothers were and that they had parted on angry terms. The kind, fun-loving uncle she remembered was a different person, angry and cross most of the time.

Sophie pushed the parmigiano, one of her favourite dishes, around her plate. Her aunt had made it especially to cheer her up. She tried to eat but the tightness in her throat made it difficult to swallow.

"Sophie, eat up."

"I am not hungry tonight. Please excuse me. I would like to go to my room."

"Are you ill?" Maria placed her hand on Sophie's forehead. "Sophie, this is your favourite."

"Leave the girl alone and stop fussing." Roberto's words came through clenched teeth.

Sophie stood at her bedroom window, close to tears. Her

uncle walked across the across the lawn and disappeared behind the pomegranate bush. She heard muffled voices. Her tears forgotten, she leaned on the thick window ledge. Uncle Roberto's strained voice pleaded, the other male voice was angry. As much as she tried, she could not hear the words. Uncle Roberto suddenly appeared from behind the tree and looked directly at her window. She jumped back as the other man disappeared into the shadows. *What was that all about?* she thought.

Life lulled easily into routine. Sophie spent the mornings with Uncle Roberto on the farm and the afternoons with Aunt Maria, working on the books. She wrote to her father daily and reported the farm was doing well. Signor Matteo had placed several large orders. She decided to omit the encounter by the pomegranate bush.

Alberto's letters were not as frequent as Sophie's, but today's letter was full of information. He confided in Sophie that Signor Matteo had written to compliment him on the quality of the silk, reassuring him that Monsieur Dubois had been dismissed as a spy. He continued:

> *This morning I hired a young gentleman, Mr. Carlos Wainwright, to be in charge of quality control and merchandising for both the farm in Lucca and the mill in Derby. He is my apprentice and I have written to Uncle Roberto asking him to teach him as much as he can about sericulture during the summer. I suggest he stay at the villa. He arrives...*

Sophie stopped reading, tears filling her eyes. How could

Father allow a stranger to stay at *their* villa. Was this apprentice her replacement? No, she thought, Papa wouldn't replace her, would he? She looked down at the letter again.

> *He arrives on Wednesday. I am acquainted with the family. His mother is Italian and his father comes from an old established merchant family. He speaks fluent Italian, English, and some French.*
>
> *I thought I should warn you that Uncle Roberto is not as enthusiastic about this gentleman. He is afraid he will interfere with the business, and Mr. Forester here at the mill has also expressed some concern. I disagree. Mr. Wainwright is a great asset to us all. Dearest Sophie, I hope I have your support. Mr. Wainwright is a clever man and a gentleman. You will learn a great deal from him, as he will learn from you.*

She placed the letter on her bedside table, feeling conflicted and wondering how to interpret her father's words. A loud bang came from the kitchen, followed by Roberto yelling, "I can't believe Alberto would do this to me!" *Oh dear*, Sophie thought, *Father was right, Uncle Roberto is not happy*. His anger was obvious, but as the panic rose in his voice, she heard fear until he finally made no sense.

Sophie went down and tried to calm him. "Perhaps Mr. Wainwright can help…" Before she could finish, he lashed out, almost hitting her. "He could be a spy and steal all our secrets or murder us in our beds."

"Don't be ridiculous, Roberto. Now calm down and don't yell at Sophie. She's trying to help," Maria intervened.

Roberto calmed a little and spoke in a normal voice. "You don't understand the implications this has. It could ruin us." He marched out of the kitchen and Sophie heard fear in his voice: *This isn't about Mr. Wainwright*, she thought. *He is scared.*

It was that time of the day when the sun glowed burnt-orange and lazily floated into the horizon; dusk promising darkness. Sophie sat under the olive tree and closed her book, the light now too dim for reading. She relished the peacefulness, the silence broken by chirping insects and scurrying lizards. She frowned as a mechanical sound came closer, invading the peace. Roberto's truck chugged to a halt outside the front door. He slammed the truck door and marched off to the shed.

Sophie stayed to get a first glimpse of Mr. Wainwright. She watched his tall frame uncurl from the truck. Much younger than she'd expected and quite handsome, his thick, wavy brown hair partially covered one side of his face. He gently pushed it away from his eyes. Aunt Maria greeted him and his smile lit up the space around him. Sophie thought she might swoon, if she were the swooning type.

"Sophie, come and meet Mr. Wainwright," called Aunt Maria.

She clung to her book and wished she had changed into a prettier dress. Mr. Wainwright was even more handsome up close. She took a breath and hoped he could not hear her pounding heart. "Welcome, Mr. Wainwright. I hope you had a pleasant journey."

"Somewhat long and tedious but not unpleasant. I can see your father was not exaggerating when he described his beautiful daughter. I am pleased to make your acquaintance, Signorina Romano." Mr. Wainwright took Sophie's hand and kissed it. Blushing, she almost gasped at his touch. Her aunt smiled and gently steered them into the living room.

Sophie could hardly remember the evening meal. Mr. Wainwright talked about his family's merchandising business and his lack of interest in it, but he did express an enthusiasm for silk farming. Uncle Roberto made some nasty comments, which went unnoticed. She offered to show the guest around the villa.

Opening the front door, Sophie forgot Mr. Wainwright's handsomeness. He was a stranger stepping into her world, a world that belonged to her, her mother and father.

"This is the kitchen, but meals are served at the farmhouse, so you won't need to cook." Her voice sounded curt. She quickly realized her mother would expect her to be courteous to a guest in their home and led the way to the bedrooms. Aunt Maria had made the bed in the guest room.

"I grew up in this house and it is very special to me and my father. Please treat it well."

Mr. Wainwright twisted his head slightly. She could see blue flecks in his grey eyes. "You don't approve of me, do you? Your father warned me about your uncle but I don't understand what I have done to displease you."

Blushing, sensing she was being reprimanded, she responded. "I am not sure of your motives, or Father's for that matter, and strangers don't belong here. Father should know that." Sophie felt her mother's disapproval—she was being rude. "I apologize. Those comments were uncalled for."

"I will treat the villa with great respect; your father mentioned how important the place is to you. He told me how clever you are and he expects you to be working as his partner soon. The mill is your inheritance."

"Papa, I mean Father, told you that?" She felt the weight of the world lifted off her shoulders. Her father still believed in her and their future was together at the mill.

"He did, and I think he is hoping we can work together."

"Definitely. But Uncle Roberto is going to be difficult."

"He needs time. When he realizes I am here to help, he will come around. May I ask you if we can use our first names? Please call me Carlos."

"Sophie. Neither my father, nor I, are big on protocol."

"Sophie, it has been a long day. I must get some rest for an early start tomorrow."

Skipping across the lawn, Sophie's heart floated. Her father still loved her and this handsome man had just dropped into her life. Passing the pomegranate bush, she heard a noise and her heart stopped. "Hello? Is someone there?"

A voice from behind said, "Sophie, what are you doing here. Get in the house." Uncle Roberto pushed her towards the house. "It's not wise for you to be out."

Sophie frowned. "I was showing Carlos his room. Aunt Maria sent me."

"Get inside. It's not safe here at night."

Sophie went straight to her room and, without putting the light on, she looked out of the window. Voices came up through the pomegranate bush and there was a scuffle. The bush shook and Uncle Roberto fell on the lawn. He quickly stood up, his arms punching wildly. A male figure ran into the shadows and Uncle Roberto came into the house. She crept to the top of the stairs. Aunt Maria's panicked voice said, "Roberto, what happened? You are covered in blood."

"Nothing. I tripped in the dark and banged my nose. I think it's broken."

"Here, hold this to stop the bleeding."

"Ouch, that hurt!"

"Those men were back, weren't they? Don't lie to me! They did this to you. Roberto, what is going on? Do you owe them money? Is that the problem?"

"Stop fussing, woman. I told you I fell."

Nothing more was said and Sophie went back to her room. She opened her writing pad: *Dearest Father, Mr. Wainwright arrived this afternoon. A pleasant man and seems eager to learn. I confess I was upset about him staying at the villa. Uncle Roberto is behaving oddly. He doesn't like Mr. Wainwright, but perhaps it will change when he gets to know him.* Sophie stared at the letter, wondering if she should tell her father about the incident. Was Uncle Roberto lying? He did fall, but she assumed the other man had hit him. And why was he running away? Too tired to finish the letter, she went to bed.

* * *

Roberto soon warmed up to Carlos. There was no doubt about his charm and knowledge. Carlos was an eager learner and a good match for Sophie, while Roberto was a good teacher. Today's lessons included the Romano method of cultivating the white mulberry tree—one of the Romano secrets. Roberto's passion had returned and she remembered her uncle tending the trees when she was a child. The high quality of the mulberry leaves translated into a fine silk thread.

Walking through the avenue of trees, Sophie felt Carlos' stare. She looked up, and he smiled and slipped his hand into hers. Her heart skipped at the warm sensation of his touch.

"Pay attention." Uncle Roberto was pointing to the pruned lower branches when Aunt Maria came running up, shouting, "Roberto, you are wanted in the office. There is a man to see you about a silk order."

Roberto nodded his head towards a worker at the end of the row. "Study what he is doing. I'll return shortly."

Carlos and Sophie walked in silence until Roberto was out of sight. Carlos slipped his arm around Sophie's waist. "I like working with you and I…" She was staring into his eyes and wondered if he was going to kiss her, but he dropped his arm and said, "Um, it's a lovely day." Sophie nodded feeling his hand brush hers as it fell to his side.

Their inspection of the mulberry leaves complete, they headed back towards the silk shed to find Roberto. Sophie stopped, causing Carlos to bump into her as she saw Roberto walk across the lawn towards a fancy car. The man at his side was Monsieur Dubois.

"Who is that man?" Carlos said.

"He's a devious businessman from Paris. He owns a silk mill in Lyon. Why is he here talking to Uncle Roberto?"

"It is normal for Roberto to meet with other mill owners to discuss business. I'll explain how business works."

"Don't patronize me, Carlos. I may be young but I understand business and that man is bad news." Furious with Carlos' comment, Sophie flounced up to her room to change for dinner. Strange sensations whirled around inside: one minute she felt rage, another tenderness, and another fear. They were all mixed up. The tenderness she felt for Carlos under the mulberry trees had been overwhelming and she was sure he felt the same. His implication that she didn't understand business had taken her back, or was it the shock of seeing Monsieur Dubois. What was *he* up to?

* * *

Carlos gave her a strange look over the dinner table. She ignored him.

"Uncle, I saw Monsieur Dubois leaving the farm this afternoon."

"He's a prospective customer. It is none of your concern."

"Uncle, he is not an honest businessman. Father has met with him before and he's the man who tried to take away the Bologna Mill's business from us."

"Don't be ridiculous, child. He is a prospective customer and you are mistaken. His name is not Dubois."

"But…"

"Enough. You are here to learn about sericulture, not to criticize who I do business with."

Sophie had been silenced. She wondered if she had been mistaken.

"Your aunt tells me you have been neglecting the bookkeeping. Tomorrow I want you to work all day in the office." Uncle Roberto was rarely adamant about anything, and this change in attitude surprised her.

"And Carlos, I would like you to go to Bologna tomorrow and meet Signor Matteo. He is our best customer with the exception of my brother at the Derby Mill. Meet me in the office after dinner to go over the orders."

* * *

Carlos left for Bologna on the early train. While Maria baked and prepared breakfast, Sophie began working in the office. The room was a mess. Roberto had scattered the Bologna invoices all over the desk. She sighed as she began gathering and filing the papers. The latest invoice for Bologna was missing and marked as unpaid in the ledger. She was sure she had entered it as paid. She thought this odd, but quickly dismissed it, assuming Roberto had sent it with Carlos.

Working in the office with Aunt Maria was trying Sophie's patience. Her aunt pretended she understood bookkeeping, but Sophie was constantly correcting her entries. This morning had been more frustrating than usual. She felt an unexplained sense of anxiety, a premonition of disaster. She shook it off, blaming the oppressive heat. She welcomed siesta time and took her book to read in the shade of the olive tree, hoping to catch a breeze. She glanced up at the blue sky. A watery haze was forming around the sun—a storm was coming. The rattling and clomping of a horse and cart disturbed the quiet. Uncle Roberto greeted two scruffy looking men who spoke in hushed words. Obviously unaware of Sophie's presence, they began loading the cart with silk bales. She didn't recognize the men and tried to think of any new customers. Something was not right. Why would anyone load silk during siesta time? The cart loaded, the horse clopped lazily along the driveway and Uncle Roberto disappeared.

About an hour later she returned to the office. Aunt Maria was already at work.

"Aunt Maria, did you write an invoice for a new customer today?"

"No, why do you ask?"

"Two men with a horse and cart just loaded bales of silk and left."

"Does Roberto know?"

"Yes. He helped them load it."

"Roberto forgot to ask us for an invoice. I'll speak to him."

"But we don't have any local customers. Who are these men?"

"Customers, of course! You ask too many questions. I'll deal with it and… you," Aunt Maria wagged her finger at Sophie, "can keep your nose out of it." Maria stared at Sophie defiantly and slid a cashbook into her desk drawer. "I have some work to do in the kitchen," she said as she took a small key out of her pocket and locked the desk drawer.

* * *

Thunder had been rumbling around the sky all evening. The air was thick with moisture and forks of brilliant white lightning followed by a sudden loud boom announced the storm finally breaking. Carlos' train was due at eight, and Uncle Roberto set off for the station just as the rain came down in torrents. Aunt Maria fussed about the roads and paced up and down the living room wringing her hands, afraid that the truck would get stuck in the mud. Sophie went to her room. She really wanted to go to the villa and wait for Carlos, but Aunt Maria would have asked questions. The storm passed and Sophie opened her eyes to the sound of a truck coming up the driveway. It was nearly midnight. The downpour must have delayed them. She peered through the window. Carlos called out good night and walked into the villa. Maria was hugging Roberto as though he'd come back from war. He shook her off, and Sophie heard him climb the stairs followed by Maria.

She waited for them to settle before she tiptoed down the stairs. She opened the front door squeezing through without the door squeaking and ran across to the villa. "Carlos, it's me. Can I come in?"

"Sophie, what are you doing here?" Carlos walked out of the bathroom, a towel around his waist. She almost cried out and sucked in an enormous breath. "Carlos, I am sorry. I'll come back later."

"No. Stay, please. I was wet and cold from pushing the truck out of mud and needed to warm up in the tub." Carlos said, walking into the bedroom. "Take a seat in the living room, I'll be out in a minute."

Sophie felt weak at the knees and was glad to sit down. The image of Carlos with wet, tousled hair and a bare chest made her heart race and she felt clammy. She wondered if she was starting a fever as her stomach swirled. She took several deep breaths to calm herself when his voice vibrated through her and she could feel the heat from her blushing cheeks.

"What brings you here at this time of night? I'm surprised Maria let you come."

"She doesn't know I'm here. I probably shouldn't be here. It isn't very proper, but I wanted to tell you what happened today." She watched him run his fingers through his wet hair. She breathed in the fragrance of fresh soap and wanted to touch him. He was speaking to her but she couldn't hear a word.

"Sophie!" he said, putting his hand on her shoulder and making her spine tingle.

"Sorry, what were you saying?"

"I was saying it was a fruitful visit to Bologna. Signor Matteo is a good businessman and thinks highly of your father but has grave concerns about your uncle. Roberto is delivering one or two silk bales short but charging him full price, and it has been going on for some time. He is pleased the quality of the silk is back to normal."

Sophie kept her head down fiddling with the sash on her dress. "Did you take an invoice to Bologna?"

"Yes, Roberto gave it to me before I left. But it was weird—it had been altered. I brought it back, I thought you could check it against the books."

Sophie told Carlos about the cart and silk bales and Aunt Maria's reaction and the locked drawer.

"Do you think those bales are the ones missing from Signor Matteo's order?"

"They might be, but why?"

"Now I know why your father has concerns about the farm operation and it makes sense. I think Roberto is caught up in some scheme. Sophie, be careful." Carlos gently brushed a stand of hair from her cheek. "I don't want anything to happen to you."

She couldn't move or speak. Her eyes fixed on his, she tried to breathe.

Carlos took her hand, she didn't resist, his arm encircled her shoulders, she could feel his heart pounding as hard as her own. His touch was electric as he gently pulled her toward him. She thought she would die as their lips touched. How much time had passed, she had no idea, she just wanted to stay in his arms forever. He kissed her again and her body filled with desire. Breaking the kiss, he looked into her eyes. "Sophie, I'm in love with you. I fell in love the first day we met."

Sophie wasn't sure about love. Were all these sensations love? She wanted to be with him and her heart felt full to overflowing, the sense of yearning all new. Was this how it felt to be in love? Carlos kissed her again more aggressively. She pulled back, realizing what he wanted.

"No, Carlos. I must go."

"Of course. I'll walk you home."

"Across the lawn?" They both laughed. Carlos gave her a peck on the cheek. "See you tomorrow."

She lay in her bed, her body trembling, as she came to the conclusion that she was truly in love with Carlos, and fell into a deep, happy sleep.

Maria Wants a Daughter

The heat of the summer waned towards the end of August. The normal farm routine plodded on during the day and everyone enjoyed the cooler evenings. Aunt Maria explained the invoicing errors to the Bologna Mill as an honest mistake. Neither Sophie nor Carlos was convinced of the honest part, but without proof there was little they could do.

Uncle Roberto kept to himself, busy with the farm, and Carlos trailed behind him, learning the art of sericulture. Aunt Maria made an effort to befriend Sophie as they worked.

"Sophie, I always envied your mother. I remember when you were born, right here on the farm. I always wanted a daughter and Roberto wanted a son, but it was not to be. When your mother died, I hoped you would come and live here with us but your father insisted you stay with him. Don't you ever wish you had a mother around?"

"I miss Mama every day. Sometimes when I'm thinking about her, I can feel her near me. Papa does too. We both feel her in the villa. Mama hated leaving here and I think she came home."

"Come home too, and be close to your mother. I'll take care of you, not that you need looking after. You are almost a grown woman. We could do things together."

"Aunt Maria, that is kind of you, but my place is with Papa. I'm going to take over the mill one day."

"What about getting married and having children? I see how you look at Carlos. You need a woman to help you. You are very young and I am afraid Carlos will break your heart one day. There are plenty of young Italian men who would treat you well and, when you are ready, we can plan your wedding together. You could raise your family at the villa and follow in your mother's footsteps. Your mother would be so proud of you. Working in a mill is no place for a young woman. I don't think your mother would approve of that."

Her aunt's words hurt, suggesting her mother's disapproval cut with the sharpness of a knife. What would her mother say? Sophie remembered her mother in the kitchen baking and cooking to entertain friends or Papa's business clients from Lucca and Bologna. Her mother had teased her about her tomboy ways when tending a scraped knee. She scrunched her shoulders, feeling her mother's hug as she gently wiped away her tears. She couldn't visualize her mother working on the farm, at the mill or in Papa's office. She felt burning tears. How she wished she could ask her mother.

"Aunt Maria, I need some fresh air; I'll be back before lunchtime."

Sophie left the office and walked over to the villa, the closest place to feel her mother. She sat at the kitchen table letting the warm tears flow down her cheeks.

"Mama, I miss you. Aunt Maria wants me to stay here, get

married and live in the villa. It is tempting. What about Papa? I want to get married and I think I am in love with Carlos, but I also want to work with Papa in the mill. Mama is it wrong? I know proper ladies don't work at jobs, especially in England. The girls at school couldn't wait to finish their studies and search for a suitable husband. Do you think I have found my husband? Mama, if I married Carlos I would be able to take over the mill. Papa would approve and I think you would too." She answered her own question; her place was at her father's side in England, and hopefully, one day, with Carlos too. She thought about Aunt Maria and was sorry to disappoint her. Sophie thought it was unfair of her aunt to expect her to fill her desperate need for a daughter. Comfortable with her decision, she opened the front door turned and said, "Thank you, Mama."

Knowing she was late for the mid-day meal Sophie was, at first, relieved to see Uncle Roberto in the yard. He was talking to a man climbing into a shiny black car. She shuddered—was that Monsieur Dubois? It was hard to tell as the car drove off. Sophie and Roberto joined Carlos and Maria at the table.

"Uncle Roberto, did I just see you talking to Monsieur Dubois? What did *he* want?"

"Stay out of my business. I told you before that man is not Monsieur Dubois."

"But, Uncle, I know…" Carlos gave Sophie a kick under the table.

Uncle Roberto puffed like a steam engine, his face bright red. She expected steam to shoot out of his ears. "Mind your own business. I think it is time you went back to your father."

"No!" Maria shouted. "Sophie is staying with us; she needs a mother."

"You are not her mother. I never intended to father children and I'm not starting now. They are trouble, and Sophie's meddling ways are all the proof I need."

Maria glared at Roberto with a palpable hatred. Sophie pulled back, waiting for Aunt Maria's response. "Are you telling me it was because of you we never had a child?"

Roberto cackled a sarcastic laugh. "And how do you think I could manage that? You're not the greatest ..." He trailed off, giving Maria a smirk.

Maria jumped up from the table, tears streaming down her face, and ran up to her bedroom. Roberto shook his head. "Women."

Sophie felt for Carlos' hand under the table. He gave it a gentle squeeze. Uncle Roberto's outburst had shocked her. He wasn't the uncle who played with her and tickled her under her chin, making her giggle when she was little. Today she realized she was afraid of him.

* * *

Later that afternoon a puffy-eyed Maria came into the office. "Sophie, ignore your uncle. He's upset about business and money right now. I want you to stay, please."

"How are you, Aunt Maria? I am so sorry he spoke to you so..." Sophie wasn't sure what to say. She felt sorry for her aunt and didn't want to add to her grief but she needed to be honest.

"I miss Mother very much and it would be nice to have you to talk to and make plans. I'm not sure about getting married, but I do love Carlos. I hope you can understand why I can't stay here. My place is with my father. I am part of his dream for the mill. Mother understood how stubborn and adventurous I was, even when I was little."

Maria Wants a Daughter

An uncomfortable silence followed and Sophie waited for a storm to break. Aunt Maria stared at her. The words that followed stunned Sophie. "Martina wins again. Your sweet, kind mother was a spoiled brat raised by a fancy family; she had everything. She swept the best brother off his feet from under my nose and gave birth to a daughter. Everyone liked her. I was left with Roberto, no children and no money. I wasn't sorry when she died. I thought I might get Alberto's respect and I could adopt you as my daughter."

"Maria, stop!" Carlos shouted from the front door. "I'm sorry. This is none of my business but you can't speak to Sophie like that—she is not to blame for your unhappiness."

Startled, Maria swung around and stared at Carlos. "You'll regret interfering. I'm going to fetch Roberto. We'll see what he has to say."

Carlos put his arms around Sophie and stroked her hair. The lump in her throat threatened to explode into sobs. She clung to him until her throat relaxed. He lifted her chin and gently kissed her lips. Nothing else mattered, the world was safe here in Carlos' arms.

"I love you Sophie, and one day I will marry you."

"Does that mean we are engaged?"

"If you say yes, I think it does."

"Yes, I will marry you, Carlos Wainwright. Let's keep it a secret until we see Father."

Maria's quest for Roberto's support had not gone well. Sophie moved closer to Carlos as Roberto yelled, "No, Sophie is not staying and I want Carlos gone too."

Maria's sobbing broke the quietness of siesta time. Sophie wanted to comfort her but she was rebuffed.

Her safe place under the olive tree branches reached out and

Sophie guided Carlos to the bench. She leaned against him, enjoying the peace. The silence broke as the gravel driveway crunched rhythmically, lazily, as a horse and cart approached.

"That's the same cart I told you about, from the day you were in Bologna."

Roberto came out of the warehouse. Carlos said, "What is he saying to those men. I can't hear him."

"I can't either, it looks as though he is instructing them to load those bales of silk. I thought he had stopped that when we discovered the Bologna Mill had been shorted. What should we do?"

Carlos thought for a minute. "Nothing. I think we need to return to England and talk to your father."

* * *

Sophie cabled her father that she and Carlos would be returning to England. They had booked a passage leaving Livorno for Southampton on September 10th, almost a week away. The atmosphere in the house was charged with anger and sadness. Aunt Maria cried every time she looked at Sophie. Uncle Roberto was sullen and argumentative but at least he'd stopped yelling at Maria. Activity was high in the silk sheds as the silk from the cocoons was ready for spinning. This part of the process was the last thing Sophie and Carlos had to learn. Perhaps because the farm was so busy, or because Roberto was afraid he was being watched, there was no further suspicious silk bale pickups, and Signor Matteo had no complaints about either deliveries or quality.

* * *

Sophie placed her trunk and bag outside the front door between the hibiscus bushes and admired the bright red and yellow flowers. She walked over to the villa, her heartstrings pulling to breaking point; she was leaving her mother. The villa felt like a warm blanket wrapping around her every time she entered. She felt safe and loved, especially in the kitchen. She sat at the kitchen table, but today she shivered; it didn't feel warm. Her mother appeared, not at the stove but sitting across from her at the table. Her smile, only slight, turned to worry. Sophie felt a gentle touch on her hands. "Mama, what is it? Something is wrong."

"Sophie, look out for your father. I can't protect him from all the evil. Tell him I am waiting for him here."

"Mama, what are you saying?"

"My darling daughter, life may not be as you expect. Stay strong. Your father has taught you well. Remember me in your heart. I love you…"

Martina began to fade, her words too soft to hear.

"Mama, please, don't go. Is Father going to die? Tell me what is going to happen. I couldn't bear to lose Papa too." She felt a kiss on her cheek and her mother was gone.

The room felt warm again, but empty. Sophie closed her eyes, willing her mother to be there when she opened them, but she was gone. Was her father going to die? Why were things not going to be as she expected? Was she talking about Carlos? She felt a tingling in her heart and smiled: "Yes, Mama, I can feel you in my heart."

The front door creaked. "Carlos?"

Carlos entered the kitchen. "Who are you talking to?"

"Saying goodbye to Mama."

"Well, it's time to go. Roberto is waiting in the truck. Is

71

something wrong?"

"I'm fine. As much as I want to leave this place, some things are hard to leave behind."

Carlos kissed her. "You're safe with me."

Troubles at the Mill

The rich green countryside filled Sophie with joy. The parched soil and intense heat of an Italian summer was behind her. Soon she would be home and with her father again. The long journey had given her time to think. She would look after her father or, she pondered, was her mother asking her to look *out* for him? And Carlos, perhaps her mother was warning her to be cautious about her engagement. The more she reflected on it, the more she agreed Papa would not approve. She refused to believe anything would happen to her father and, not having any particular expectations beyond working at the mill, there was nothing to go wrong. She still had a sense of foreboding, but today she was too excited to pay it much attention.

The train began to slow down and the maze of Derby's railway tracks came into view, replacing the lush green farmland with grey industry. Sophie lifted the strap to open the window and put her head out. Catching soot in her eye, she quickly pulled her head back inside. Carlos took the corner of his handkerchief and removed the ash. She felt his warmth and they kissed. "Carlos, I don't think we should tell father about us. Not yet anyway."

"I agree. He will say that you are too young. We can wait a while." The conversation was cut short as the train came to a halt. She saw her father waving. She ran to his open arms: "I'm home."

"I'm happy you are home. I missed you so much." He led her out of the station. Dalton was standing beside the open door of a big black car.

"Papa—oh, I mean Father—you bought a car. It is very elite."

"Very nice, sir," Carlos added.

"We'll take you home first, Carlos. You can travel in the front. I'll sit with Sophie in the back."

Half an hour later, Dalton drove the car down the long, poplar-lined driveway to Oak House. Glancing at her father she said, "I finally said goodbye to Lucca."

"I felt the same way when I came back here. I said goodbye to your mother, knowing she was happy at the villa. This is our home now."

Mrs. Simpson greeted them at the door and Dalton unloaded Sophie's luggage. She walked down to the river and gazed across at the Romano Silk Mill, steam billowing from the tall chimney. Italy seemed in another world. Uncle Roberto and Aunt Maria came to mind, and she was uncertain of how to tell her father about the strange happenings at the farm. *That can wait until tomorrow*, she thought, walking back to the house.

She unpacked her bags and placed the few things she had bought as presents on her dresser. Her fingers traced her father's initials engraved in gold on the side of a leather case. Putting it to one side, she decided to give it to him at dinner;

she loved giving presents. She went downstairs to the kitchen. Cook was grumpy. She didn't like being disturbed close to dinnertime. "Miss Sophie, welcome home. What can I do for you?" Cook was always polite but the pursed lips and frown didn't fool Sophie.

"Put down your pot for one second, I have a surprise for you."

"Miss Sophie, I don't have time for games." Cook sighed and set the pot on the stove.

Sophie placed a package in the palm of her hands. "A little present from Bologna, Italy, for you."

Cook's lips curled gently at the corners. Glancing at the wrapped package, she pulled the ribbon. Her round, chubby face broke into a smile as a string of colourful beads appeared. "They are beautiful, Miss Sophie. Thank you." She held them up just as Mrs. Simpson came into the kitchen.

"What is going on? Something is burning on the stove."

Cook grabbed the handle of the pot. "I'm sorry, it was my fault Mrs. Simpson." Sophie handed her a package. "I brought this for you from the silk mill in Bologna. It is the finest silk in all of Europe, made from the Romano silkworms."

"Thank you." Mrs. Simpson gasped at the delicate, veil-like shawl shimmering in the light. The pink and violet colours contrasted brightly against her dark dress. Happy that her presents had been well received, and with one last present in hand, Sophie went into the dining room to find Dalton.

"Miss Sophie, dinner isn't quite ready."

"I have something for you, Dalton." She handed him a package loosely wrapped in cloth. She had decided a ribbon was perhaps not appropriate for Dalton, making it easy for the white silk scarf to slide out of the package. Dalton caught it, and glanced at Sophie, puzzled. " Miss Sophie! For me?"

"You don't like it." Suddenly she was afraid she had insulted Dalton.

"It is a fine scarf, finer than I have ever seen or had the pleasure to wear." Dalton's face lit up, his eyes filled with kindness and appreciation. "Thank you. I don't quite know what to say. Miss Sophie, you are very kind."

When Sophie arrived for dinner, her father was already at the table. Carrying her father's present behind her back, she sidled into the room. "Father, a present for you from Italy." She held the briefcase up and handed it to her father.

"It's magnificent. Such fine Italian leather, and my initials too. Thank you. I shall put it to good use." Alberto stood up and hugged his daughter. "It's wonderful to have you home."

"I missed you. If it wasn't for Carlos' company, I think I would have gone mad. Uncle Roberto has changed. He was grouchy and angry most of the time. Aunt Maria is a strange woman, always fussing, and I worry about her keeping the books." Sophie hesitated, wondering if she should convey her suspicions about Roberto giving away bales of silk. She decided to enjoy her first night back, she'd tell him tomorrow. She knew he would be disappointed and didn't want to spoil their first night together. Besides, she wanted Carlos to be with her.

"Did you learn sericulture and silk spinning?"

"Carlos and I learned together when I wasn't working on the books. Aunt Maria thinks it is unladylike to work in the mill. She said Mama wouldn't approve."

"Don't listen to your aunt. She always resented your mother, and I can assure you that your mother would be very proud of you. What do you think of Carlos?"

Sophie could feel her cheeks burn. "He's intelligent and works hard and is committed to Romano Silk. Uncle Roberto didn't complain and Signor Matteo thought highly of him."

"Do I see a little blush?" Alberto studied Sophie, making her blush even more.

Sophie giggled. "A school girl crush. He is very handsome, Father."

"As long as it is no more, Sophie. You are sixteen, far too young for anything serious. About this I know your mother would agree with me."

"Yes, Papa." Taking a deep breath, Sophie was relieved when Dalton began to serve dinner.

"Sophie, I had hoped you would start secretarial school when you returned from Italy but the Michaelmas term has already started. Why don't you start working at the mill while you wait for the next session to start?"

Sophie tried not to sound too excited. "That's a great idea. I'll come with you to the mill in the morning."

* * *

Sophie met with Mr. Young, who seemed delighted to have an assistant. He gave her a desk and she started work. The thought of being near Carlos on a daily basis pleased her. She could see Carlos talking to her father. He turned and smiled and then frowned before leaving the meeting. He deliberately walked close to her desk and touched her hand, sending a tingling sensation up her arm and a blush to her cheeks. After lunch Carlos moved close to her desk and pushed a note into her hand. She giggled, causing Mr. Young to glanced up from his work. She smiled and excused herself. The note said, *Meet me by the river in half an hour. C.*

The mill machinery clanged loudly as she walked through

the factory floor. She heard her father's voice shouting over the noise to Mr. Forester. She slipped out unseen, hurried down the path and saw Carlos waiting for her. It was a beautiful warm autumn day, for which she was thankful as she had come without her coat. She glanced briefly over her shoulder as Carlos pulled her into his arms and whispered in her ear, sending shivers to her heart. Standing on tiptoe she reached up to kiss him. He shook his head. "No, your father might see us. He politely told me to stay away until you are old enough to start courting."

"When did he say that? We only arrived home yesterday?"

"When you were talking to Mr. Young this morning. What did you say to him?"

"I said I had a school girl crush because you are so handsome."

"Come, let's walk along the river bank."

They walked in silence. Sophie watched the mallard ducks quacking at the shoreline, expecting any passers-by to throw breadcrumbs.

"Carlos, why did you want to see me?"

"Because I miss you. I wish we could tell your father. I also wanted to ask you if you had told him about Roberto and Monsieur Dubois."

"No, I haven't. I didn't want to spoil my first night home and I would like you to be there and tell him what you saw too. Why do you ask?"

"I overheard something today. I think there is a plot against your father, and I think Mr. Forester is the ring leader."

"Plot?"

"He gets the workers all riled up about nothing. Your father fired a man, O'Reilly, for being drunk on the job. Forester told the workers it was unfair and they had better watch out for their jobs. He knows your father had no choice. The man could have been hurt. It was the next thing he said that surprised me."

"What else did Forester say?"

"He said, 'changes are coming to the mill when it merges with Lyon.' I am assuming he was talking about Monsieur Dubois."

"Could you have misheard?"

"I don't think so. I think your father should know. I am afraid to say anything at the mill in case Mr. Forester, or anyone else for that matter, overhears. He is a dangerous man with a violent temper."

"Come to the house for dinner tonight. We can tell father about what we observed in Lucca and what you heard at the mill. I'll wait until we get home to tell him you are joining us. Cook always makes more food than we can eat."

Carlos looked around, they were standing under an embankment, hidden from the mill. His hand cupped her chin. "My beautiful Sophie." She felt his warm breath on her cheeks as he bent to kiss her, feeling the urgency of his soft lips and a desire so intense it captured her breath. Carlos relaxed his lips and brushed his forehead on hers, staring into her eyes. Wishing the moment would never end, she tried to kiss him again. Carlos held her at arms length. "We must get back to work," he panted, trying to get his breath back. "Walk back to the mill. If anyone sees you, they'll think you just went for a walk. I'll walk around the mill, inspecting the wheel or something."

"Carlos."

"Go now before we do something we'll regret."

Sophie stared at the mallards swimming alongside her and struggled to calm her breath. The kiss lingered on her lips and his touch filled her heart; she was ready to succumb. Why had he pushed her away?

"Sophie! What are you doing here?" She looked up and saw her father walking to the river. Now she knew why Carlos had pushed her away and disappeared.

"I needed some air, Father. Staring at the ledger all day gets monotonous and it is a beautiful day. But I need to get back to work or Mr. Young will chastise me." Sophie guided her father up the embankment to the mill, hoping Carlos was out of sight.

"Why are you outside?"

"I, too, needed some air and time to think."

"Is something wrong?" Caught up in her emotions, she hadn't noticed his worried face.

"The mill workers seem unhappy, even militant, and I don't know why. I treat them well. I know they are upset because I fired O'Reilly, but he was a danger to himself and the other workers and no number of warnings would stop his drinking."

Was this the time to tell her father? She glanced around. There were men working on the water wheel. It would have to wait.

* * *

Sophie left the mill early and immediately went to the kitchen to warn cook there would be a guest for dinner. Cook huffed and tut-tutted but agreed that it was possible. Mrs. Simpson frowned as she listened to Sophie's instructions.

"Miss Sophie, what is this about?"

"We have a guest for dinner. Would you help me dress?"

Mrs. Simpson raised an eyebrow and smiled. "Of course, Miss Sophie."

She helped Sophie pull her corset, something she avoided wearing as much as possible. She chose an emerald green silk dress that she had bought in Lucca and wished it had a lower neckline. Aunt Maria had insisted she buy a dress that buttoned to her neck. But it nipped her tiny waist and the silk flowed to her ankles. Mrs. Simpson pinned her hair. Standing back and admiring the little girl transformed into a young woman, she said "Beautiful, Miss Sophie. I assume our guest is a young man?"

"Yes, it is Carlos."

She heard her father's voice talking to Dalton, who referred to a guest for dinner, which would be delayed upon Miss Sophie's instructions.

Sophie began to run downstairs and stopped, lifting her gown and taking one step at a time, she said, "Father, I can explain. We have a guest for dinner and I ordered it to be served later."

"Sophie, what is going on?" He stopped and audibly gasped. "Oh, Sophie!" Emotion filled his face and moisture clung to his eyelids. "So grown up and the image of your mother."

"I am grown up, Father. I invited Carlos for dinner. I'm sorry I didn't ask you, but this can't wait. We were afraid of being overheard if we spoke at the mill. Carlos has something to tell you."

"I have spoken to Carlos and asked him to leave you alone. You are far to young for romantic notions. I will not..."

"This has nothing to do with my feelings for Carlos, although I do think you are being unfair."

"My mind is made up on this subject."

Sophie followed her father into his study. Dalton poured him a sherry and discreetly left the room.

"Father, listen. This is far more serious and it has to do with the farm and the mill."

Dalton appeared again. "Mr. Wainwright to see you, sir."

Alberto sighed and glanced at his daughter. "Show him in, Dalton."

Before Carlos could say a word, Alberto began, "Carlos, I thought I expressed my concerns about you courting my daughter."

"Yes sir!" Carlos hesitated he couldn't take his eyes off Sophie. "Sophie, you look…beautiful."

"Good evening, Carlos. How nice of you to join us." She smiled, proud of her formal greeting and hoping her father would think her old enough to be a hostess and maybe to court Carlos.

Alberto cleared his throat. She smiled, seeing her father uncertain of what to say. "I…um…stand by my decision."

Carlos, also taken off guard, took a deep breath. "My visit has to do with something I overheard at the mill and some observations Sophie and I made at the farm."

The little group sat in front of the fire and Sophie explained all she had seen. The bales of silk, the short orders to Signor Matteo, the strange men fighting with Roberto, and Roberto denying Monsieur Dubois' frequent visits to the farm.

"Why didn't you tell me about this sooner?"

"Father, I wasn't sure about it. Uncle Roberto is always so bad tempered. I had the impression he owed money and Aunt Maria said not to worry about it but she kept a separate cash book in a locked drawer."

"Carlos, do you agree with this?"

"Yes, sir. Like Sophie, I wasn't sure until today when I overheard Mr. Forester, say 'things would change when Lyon takes over.' Sir, Mr. Forester incites the workers by convincing them that you are not a fair employer."

Alberto began pacing the room. "I know. I don't understand

why even my most trusted workers seem to believe his lies. I suspected a connection between Forester and Monsieur Dubois some years ago but I dismissed it at the time. Obviously there *is* a connection. I find it disturbing that he is following me; first here, then the farm and the Bologna Silk Mill. Your comments about Lucca are valid. I received a letter from Signor Matteo to say his orders are short, the quality of the silk has deteriorated and he has to challenge every invoice."

Alberto went to his desk and handed Carlos a letter. "Letters from Roberto are glowing accounts of how well the farm is doing, including false profit reports. My brother must think I'm a fool—the statements he sends don't add up." He pulled another folder from his desk and handed it to Sophie. "Are these numbers the same as those you were working on?"

Alberto continued to pace and his hushed, rhythmic footsteps filled the now quiet room. Sophie thought of her mother's words, 'look after your father.' Did she mean to protect him from these business spies? What could she do? She sensed terrible consequences. Looking up from the statement, she glanced at Carlos. His face was serious and his eyes troubled.

"Father, this statement is false. These are not the numbers I was just working on before I left Italy. Aunt Maria's inability to enter the books correctly, and her attempt to cover her mistakes and delete entries is obvious. I suspect Uncle Roberto told her to delete some entries, which have made this laughable. I think I can reconstruct some of the numbers—that would give us an idea of how bad the situation is."

Over dinner, the trio decided to find out more about Mr. Forester's past. Sophie would reconstruct the statements from the farm and Alberto would call a meeting of all the workers and meet with anyone with a grievance. If necessary, Mr. Forester would be fired.

Who is Mr. Forester?

Mr. Forester knocked on Carlos' office door. "Come in," Carlos called, closing the folder he was reading. Forester glanced at the folder. "Why are you looking at my work history?"

"I'm not. I'm looking for information for payroll. As you are here, I can ask you. It seems your date of birth is missing and Mr. Young requires it for his new record system. What is it you came to see me about?"

"Oh, it can wait. I'll see Mr. Young now."

Carlos returned the folder to the cabinet, hoping that Mr. Young would recognize his reference to a new system was in fact a ploy for information from Forester. He could feel Forester's eyes boring into his back as he closed the cabinet draw. The excuse of needing his date of birth was rather lame. Taking a much-needed gasp of air, he ran down the stairs to the mill floor to find Alberto. Sid Forester had never disclosed anything personal: his records showed no previous address or next of kin. Other than a reference from Macclesfield it was as though he didn't exist. Who was Sid Forester?

Carlos found Alberto in the warehouse. "Forester just caught me looking at his file. I think I covered well. I can't telephone from the office, so with your permission I'm going to Macclesfield in person. That's his last known place of employment."

"Mr. Young was satisfied when we hired him, but a visit might reveal something we don't know."

The journey to Macclesfield took Carlos longer than expected. Driving over the Derbyshire dales along the winding roads, some no better than dirt farm tracks, was slow going. He couldn't help but admire the rolling hills and craggy, almost barren hillcrests. The sun setting and the light moving from dusk to semi-darkness gave the undulating dales a sense of movement. By the time he reached Macclesfield, the office was closed. Thirsty and hungry, the Pheasant & Duck pub looked inviting and it advertised rooms for travellers.

Carlos ordered a pint of ale and steak and kidney pie. He glanced round the bar at the patrons and asked the barman, "Know anything about the mill across the road."

"Not much, but those lads at the table in the corner work there. Ask them." The barman yelled, "Hey, Charlie! This fellow is asking about the mill."

Carlos introduced himself as working at the mill in Derby. As a fellow mill worker he was invited to join the table. The conversation hushed as several plates of steak and kidney pie arrived. Between mouthfuls, Carlos commented, "This is the best pie." The men all laughed and Carlos added, trying to break his cultured speech, "Best steak and kidney I've cum across. Better than mi mam's. I wouldna' tell 'er that." Laughter shook the table.

"So what brings y'u to these parts?" Charlie asked.

Carlos panicked; he didn't have a story. He concentrated on eating, gesturing with hand to mouth that the pie was hot and he couldn't speak, giving himself time to think.

"I'm getting married and mi wife-to-be is from around here and wants to live near her ma and pa." Carlos rolled his eyes. "Not sure about moving. I have a good job at the Romano Mill but the floor foreman, Forester, said he worked here a while back and it was a good place to work."

The men all shook their heads. "I don't know that name. It might be a different mill, there's two in Macclesfield."

Charlie frowned. "Y'u know there were a fellow work 'ere a while back, 'e said he were going to work in Derby. He 'ad a foreign sounding name. It weren't Forester. Troublemaker he were, glad to be rid of him. Now I remember. Sid, Sid Dobos. He 'ated being called that but I couldna pronounce the French way."

Carlos choked on his ale, hardly getting his breath, Charlie was slapping him on the back. "Y'u okay mate?"

Carlos nodded, carefully taking a sip from his glass. "Thanks. Almost went down the wrong way."

Charlie stood up. "Nice talking to y'u Carlos. I have to go meet the wife. Women's Institute meeting tonight, she likes me to walk 'er home from church 'all."

* * *

The drive back across the Derbyshire dales took Carlos all day. The rain came down in torrents and the car had gotten stuck in the mud three times. It was past ten when he arrived back at the mill. He was surprised to see lights on, since the evening shift finished at nine. He heard voices from the mill floor.

Davies stood at the door and put his hand up. "Mr. Wainwright, I don't like this. Forester is stirring the men up."

"What for?" Carlos peered round the corner and estimated there were fifty workers crammed on the factory floor. Forester voice boomed over the murmuring crowd, "I know Mr. Romano has made promises to some of you. I ask you, do you believe him? He's a toff, scum who exploits workers; they're all the same. Fancy talkers, sitting in their big houses, while you scrape a living." There was a pause and a slight rumble of voices. "What! Are you spineless? Mill owners don't care about you, they want profit." There were a few more muffled comments. "We have to stand together to get decent wages and conditions."

Someone yelled, "Mr. Romano pays us well and the conditions are good compared to some." A louder cheer went up hesitantly.

Forester tried yelling over the speaker. "They don't care about you or your families. Remember what happened to O'Reilly. His family is in the workhouse, his wife on the street. Do you want that to happen to you?" The cheers were louder. We need to support our brothers. I say we strike until O'Reilly is reinstated." The room was silent.

Someone from the back of the room yelled, "I can't afford to strike with a wife and four youngn's." Heads nodded and three women pushed to the front. A well-rounded woman pulled her shawl around her and said, "O'Reilly were a drunk and deserved what he got. What's in it for you, mister? Mr. Romano treats us good." The other two yelled, "Better 'an you." Laughter and a rumble of agreement went round the room. Forester tried to shout over the heightening chattering as the workers ignored him and began leaving the floor; they nodded to Carlos and Davies who had moved onto the floor.

"What's going on here? Why are all these workers here at this time of night?" Carlos shouted.

Forester shrugged. "I could ask you the same."

"I was returning Mr. Romano's automobile." Carlos thought it wise not to let Forester know he had heard his speech. He grabbed Forester's arm. "What are you up to?" Forester shrugged his arm loose. "Get your hands off me. I'm the foreman and I needed to talk to the men and women." Forester glanced at Davies. "I speak up for my fellow brothers. Not like him." Forester flipped his head towards Davies and pushed past Carlos and left the mill.

Carlos told the night watchman not let anyone in the mill until morning shift arrived. The rain had started again, so he took the car and dropped Davies off at his home and drove to Oak House to relay the evening's events.

* * *

"Mr. Romano, I am convinced Sid Dubois in Macclesfield and Sid Forester are the same person and that he has some connection to Monsieur Dubois. A spy in our midst perhaps?"

"I agree. I spoke with several workers today. It seems Forester plants false information about my leadership and motives. Some of the men are inclined to believe his lies, fearing for their jobs. The women don't believe his lies but he threatens them, letting them believe he can harm their children." Alberto poured brandy and handed a glass to Carlos.

"He was attempting to incite strike action tonight. The workers didn't listen, in fact they supported you as a good owner. This time they walked away, but for how long? He is a good orator." Carlos sipped the brandy, glad of its warmth.

"I have never liked the way he treats the women. I witnessed him threatening one of the weavers. He covered up of course, but there is something about that man that bothers me. I spoke to the police chief, but no crime has been committed. Unfortunately, there is nothing we can do. The chief agreed to find out more about Forester and strongly suggested he be terminated."

"Sir, I agree. Perhaps the police can find out the connection between him and Dubois."

"Where am I going to find a new foreman? Terminating Forester leaves a gap, but I can't afford to keep him either." Alberto downed his brandy in one gulp. "There is one man I've been watching, Tommy Jones. He used to be a foreman in the mines in Wales and moved up here after a mining accident. I think he can do the job. I need reassurance on his loyalty."

"It would be my pleasure. I think it was Tommy Jones who stood up to Forester tonight." Carlos said

"Excellent. We'll terminate Mr. Forester tomorrow." Alberto nodded with satisfaction.

* * *

Alberto was not looking forward to meeting with Sid Forester, but the mill had to be rid of this man. He greeted the workers as he walked through the floor to the office and gestured to Forester to follow him up to the office.

"Mr. Forester, it has come to my attention that you are not satisfied with your work here. I am disappointed, as with the right attitude you could have made a good foreman. However, after speaking with the workers I discovered your methods of discipline are cruel and unwarranted. I find it necessary to terminate your employment without reference. Mr. Young has determined what we own you in wages and I expect you to leave immediately."

The silence was charged to the point of exploding. Forester said nothing, his face purple, his mouth opened without sound. The tumblers on the safe sounded like firecrackers as Mr. Young clicked the dial. His fingers slipped, making him repeat the sequence. Finally, the safe opened and he began counting pound notes.

Sophie entered. "Good morn..."

Alberto stiffened. He had forgotten Sophie would be coming to work. "Sophie, can you wait outside?"

"What's going on?" She glanced at the three men and, sensing trouble, she backed towards the door.

Forester pounced and his arm twisted around Sophie's neck, the movement so fast she didn't see it coming. She felt the cold metal of a knife touch her neck. Forester briefly pointed the knife at Alberto and returned it to Sophie's neck. "Make one move and I'll kill your precious little daughter. Now, you," the knife pointed at Mr. Young, "open the safe, never mind my wages, I'll take it all."

Sophie dared not breathe. She looked at her father, who nodded at Mr. Young to open the safe. Her father's face changed as he looked beyond her and he shook his head very slightly. Was someone behind her? Mr. Young held out several wads of notes. She felt Forester hesitate; he couldn't take the cash without letting go of either her or the knife. In that split second, Carlos, who, was standing in the doorway seized Foresters arm and shook the knife loose. Releasing Sophie,

Forester grabbed the money and ran out yelling, "You'll pay for this!"

Alberto lunged forward and embraced Sophie. His cheek on her head, he whispered, "I thought I'd lost you." She hugged him even tighter. The whole room took a deep breath. Reluctantly, Alberto released Sophie.

"Carlos, I don't know what to say. You saved Sophie's life."

"I don't think he would have carried out his threat. He got what he wanted—money."

"Mr. Young, how much money did he get?"

"Not much. In his haste he only took about £10 and he left his wages." Mr. Young lifted an envelope from the desk. "I'll call the police. He may try to return."

"I'm happy we are rid of the man. Carlos, you and I need to address the mill floor. But first I want to speak to Tommy Jones."

"I'll fetch him sir."

* * *

Alberto sat in his office staring across the river Derwent, his daughter's life flashing before him. Martina's lovely face appeared in a wispy cloud and he felt a deep sense of guilt. Martina would never forgive him if something happened to Sophie. He harboured enough guilt. Perhaps if they had stayed in Lucca, Martina would be alive. He thought about Carlos and Sophie. Carlos came from a good family and, whether he worked for the Romano mill or his father, he would provide Sophie with a good home. He thought with pride of his ambitious daughter and realized he was being selfish. A woman's place was in the home protected by a good husband.

Should he give them his blessing? But, he thought, sixteen is so young. Engrossed in his thoughts, he didn't hear Carlos tap on his door.

"Excuse me, sir. The police just arrived. I asked Tommy to wait."

Alberto gave Carlos a blank look. He had completely forgotten that Mr. Young had called the police and that he'd asked to see Tommy Jones.

"Sir!" Carlos moved to the desk. "Are you alright, sir?"

"No, I'm not alright. Someone tried to kill my daughter. Have the police arrived…"

"That's what I'm trying to tell you, sir. The chief inspector is here to see you."

Before Alberto could answer, the chief inspector and a uniformed constable walked into his office. "

"Mr. Romano, I understand there has been an incident here involving Sid Forester."

"An unpleasant business. I had called him to my office to fire him. In retaliation he attacked my daughter and stole some money."

"By coincidence, I was on my way here to arrest Mr. Forester when your call came into the station. Mr. Forester is not who he says he is. His name is Sidney Dubois—he's wanted by the French authorities for robbery and murder. My initial inquiries happened to coincide with an international bulletin I received this morning and I recognized his picture."

Alberto described what happened in the office. "He can't have gone far and he only stole £10 and didn't pick up his wages."

"He's a dangerous man. Your daughter could have been killed."

"I know that only too well. And if ever I come across him

again, I can assure you, Inspector, he will pay for threatening Sophie." Alberto felt a surge of anger mixed with guilt as the inspector referred to Sophie being killed.

"Do you have any idea where he went?"

"No."

"I'll post a constable on site. He may return for more money. Do I have your permission to search the grounds?"

"Of course. Whatever you need."

Investigations

Staring out of the window, Alberto watched the inspector giving orders to uniformed policemen. He rubbed his hand over his face and pulled his pocket watch from his waistcoat: ten o'clock, the day had only just begun and he felt exhausted.

"Sir, Tommy Jones to see you." A tall skinny man, limping slightly, walked hesitantly towards Alberto's desk.

"You wanted to see me, sir?" Tommy was holding his cap and nervously twisting the rim between his fingers.

"Mr. Jones, I am sure you are aware that Mr. Forester has left our employ and we have since discovered that he is a criminal, which explains the presence of the police."

"I do' know naught. I tried to keep out of his way."

"Mr. Jones, take a seat. When you first came to work here you told Mr. Young that prior to your accident you had been a foreman."

"Yes sir, but they said I couldn't work with a gammy leg."

"How would you like the position of foreman here at the mill?

Do you think you are up to the job?"

"Me, sir?"

"You are a good worker and your gammy leg does not impede your work here. Can you lead the workers and keep production up? And of course you will have a considerable rise in wages."

"I can do mi best, I won't let y'u down, sir." Tommy Jones hesitated. "My way of doing things is different from Mr. Forester. I don't threaten or…"

"I want the workers treated well. I do not condone Mr. Forester's methods but discipline is important. You may start your new duties as soon as I announce the changes."

"Thank you, sir. Mi wife'll be pleased; she just gave birth to another little'n, and that makes four mouths to feed."

Pleased with his decision, Alberto wondered how these men managed to provide for their families. Four children! He knew some of the women in the mill worked all day, leaving children in the care of neighbours or grandmothers. He resolved to learn more about their lives and help where he could—a good project for Sophie, he thought.

Alberto approached Sophie's desk. She looked pale and distracted. The guilt of exposing Sophie to such danger was eating at him. "I want you to go home. The inspector thinks Forester might come back for more money."

"No, Father. I want to stay here."

"My dear, that was quite an ordeal. I'll have Carlos drive you home. You are to stay in the house and tell Dalton to lock all the doors."

"Father, no."

"I insist. You'll do as I say. Pick up your things and I'll see you at dinner tonight."

* * *

As the car pulled up to Oak house, Dalton appeared. "Is something wrong, Miss Sophie?"

Sophie barged past him into the hall. "My father thinks I am a child." Dalton raised an eyebrow and glanced at Carlos, who was now standing next to him.

"What is going on here?" Mrs. Simpson called. "Miss Sophie are you ill? You are very pale."

"I'm fine."

Carlos responded, "There has been an unpleasant incident at the mill and Miss Sophie was threatened. Mr. Romano thought it best that she come home. Dalton, he instructs you to close and lock all the doors and not to let anyone into the house." Carlos continued to explain the events at the mill.

Mrs. Simpson gasped, her hand on her mouth. Quickly composing herself, she guided Sophie to the drawing room. Dalton's stance didn't change and he pulled the bell to summon the maid. "Tea for Miss Sophie."

Whispering, Dalton and Carlos left the room. Mrs. Simpson stirred two heaping spoons of sugar into the tea and handed it to Sophie.

"I don't know what all the fuss is about. I'm fine," Sophie fumed. The teacup rattled on her saucer. She held her breath, trying to calm her shaking hands. Bringing the cup to her lips, some tea spilled on her blouse and she placed the cup back on the saucer.

"Miss Sophie, you've had a shock." Mrs. Simpson took her hands and squeezed them. Sophie felt her insides shake and couldn't stop tears running down her cheeks. "I was so afraid."

"You're safe now." Mrs. Simpson let her cry.

Sophie rested most of the day, Mrs. Simpson and Dalton watching her like a hawk.

Hearing her father, she ran to greet him. She stopped, taken aback by the deeply-creased lines on his forehead, his face the colour of parchment. "Father, has something else happened?" He didn't answer her. Handing his coat and hat to Dalton he walked into his study and poured himself a brandy, downing it in one gulp.

"I need to be alone. It has been a difficult day. I have invited Carlos to join us for dinner."

"You'll be comfortable in the drawing room, Miss Sophie. I will show Mr. Wainwright in as soon as he arrives." Dalton understood Sophie's hurt. Whatever had happened at the mill was not good, she thought; even more traumatic than the morning events, if that was possible. She looked down at her plain skirt and blouse and decided to change. As she opened the door she bumped into Dalton. "Pardon me, Miss Sophie. Mr. Wainwright to see you." Dalton opened the door fully and Carlos walked in.

"Carlos, what happened at the mill after I left today? I've never seen father so worried."

"He received another letter from Signor Matteo terminating all silk orders from the Romano farm based on poor quality and inconsistent delivery. He went on to say he had received alarming news from Monsieur Dubois regarding the Romano farm. I am to leave for Bologna tomorrow morning in an attempt to save the account."

"Why isn't Father going?"

"He's worried—about you and the mill. With no order from Bologna he has suspended the evening shift and is afraid of trouble from the workers. Forester is on the loose and may try to sabotage the mill or harm you. Tommy Jones, the new foreman, needs some guidance. When I return, your father intends go to Lucca and find out what is happening at the farm."

"I know you and father can sort this out. Seeing Father so upset makes me think there is more to all this."

"That's all I know; although I did see your father in deep conversation with the inspector. I thought perhaps they had found Forester."

Alberto joined them in the drawing room. "I trust you explained to Sophie why you are going to Bologna."

"Yes, sir."

"I want you to add a trip to Lucca. First, make sure Signor Matteo is happy and then travel to the farm to make sure everything is running well. I have cabled Roberto. I received a strange telephone call threatening to destroy the farm. The inspector thinks it's a ploy to frighten us—possibly Forester taunting us. I need first hand information." Alberto tried to smile and placed his arm around Sophie. "Come, Sophie, I'm hungry." He led the way into the dining room.

"I don't want you at the mill until Forester has been found. I think you would do well to stay here and learn from Mrs. Simpson. It is important that you learn how to run a household for when you marry." Sophie flipped her gaze from her father to Carlos. "Father, are you saying I can't work at the mill?"

"I'm wondering what your mother would say, and perhaps it is time to think about marriage."

"But you said we were too young." Puzzled and not sure if she should be excited at her father's change of heart or angry that he didn't want her to work with him. Sophie tried to read Carlo's face, which appeared cold. Then it occurred to her,

Carlos had made no attempt to kiss her or touch her in the drawing room. She wondered what had changed.

At the end of the evening Carlos lingered on his way out of the door, waiting for Alberto to retreat to his study and Dalton to discreetly excuse himself. Carlos held her tightly and his kiss was intense. She whispered, "Is father giving us his blessing?" She felt his grip tighten, it felt desperate, she sensed something…she didn't know what. Carlos whispered, "Maybe. We'll talk when I get back from Italy. I'm meeting my father in London on my way." He kissed her again. "I must go, a long day tomorrow. Stay safe, I'll always love you," he hesitated, "no matter what transpires."

Sophie stood in the hall staring at the closed door. She heard Dalton's quiet footsteps. "It's time to lock up, Miss Sophie."

"Yes, of course."

"Things will work out for the best Miss Sophie, I'll make sure of that."

She frowned: everyone was talking in riddles tonight. "Good night Dalton, I'm turning in. Father is in his study."

* * *

Stretching until her fingers hit the headboard, Sophie was enjoying an extra hour in bed for the fourth day in a row and she was already bored. Pangs of hunger prompted her to dress and find out what was for breakfast. She sighed and wondered what Mrs. Simpson had in store for her today.

Surprised to see her father eating breakfast and reading the newspaper. "Father, you are late this morning."

"Good morning, I am meeting the chief inspector here. He has information and doesn't want us overheard at the mill."

100

Sophie poured some coffee and helped herself to eggs and bacon. Dalton arrived with a fresh batch of hot toast just as the front door bell rang.

The chief inspector walked into the dining room. He was a small man, immaculately dressed, with grey hair and a neatly trimmed grey mustache that fit tightly under his nose.

"Good morning, Mr. Romano, Miss Sophie." He nodded and took a seat at the table.

"Good morning, Inspector. Would you like breakfast?"

"No thank you." He nodded at Dalton who poured him a coffee.

"I have some news about Forester. I am sorry to say we have not apprehended him yet. But rest assured, he will be in jail tonight. The Sussex police have a trace on him. They believe he is heading towards the coast. All ports are on high alert."

"Does that mean I can go back to the mill? Please, Father, I'm bored."

"We'll talk about this later." Alberto frowned at Sophie's poor manners.

"Chief Inspector, this is good news. Are you quite sure we are safe?"

"Most certainly. Every police force in England is looking for him. He has probably already been arrested. There is one other thing. During our investigation we encountered a Monsieur Pierre Dubois, a Frenchman who owns a silk mill in Lyon, France. Do you know this man?"

"Yes, he came to the mill on the pretense of purchasing silk. He also went to the farm in Lucca and to one of my customers in Bologna. I don't know much about him except he is a dishonest businessman intent on spying on other silk merchants. Mr. Wainwright is currently in Italy investigating some problems that may involve Dubois."

"A man to be reckoned with." The chief inspector rubbed his chin. "But as far as I know he has not broken the law in England."

"I will make sure he is 'reckoned with,' Inspector."

"Be careful. Taking the law into your own hands is dangerous. I suspect Sid Forester, alias Dubois, is related to this man, but we haven't found the connection yet."

The inspector stood up, placing his hat on his head. "Good day, sir."

The Calm Before the Storm

Alberto reluctantly agreed to let Sophie return to work at the mill in the afternoons, as long as he escorted her. During the mornings she continued to work with Mrs. Simpson.

Sophie surprised herself. Learning to be the lady of the house wasn't all bad. She actually enjoyed it. She learned how to order daily meals and discuss menus with Cook. Mrs. Simpson explained the role of housekeeper in both a small and large house. She had difficulty understanding why the lady of the house could not make friends with the staff. Sophie liked the idea of entertaining and enjoyed the week's lesson on planning a dinner party. She thought about Carlos. His family entertained, although she noted she had never been invited. When they were married she would entertain her mother-in-law and make Carlos proud of her.

* * *

At one o'clock Alberto came home and joined Sophie for lunch and then together they returned to the mill.

"Father, I would like to give a dinner party. I thought when Carlos returns we could invite Mr. and Mrs. Wainwright and some of your business people."

Alberto smiled. "That sounds a little ambitious. Your mother gave dinner parties and I always marvelled at how she put it all together. Perhaps you should start small. I'll speak to Mrs. Simpson. I think it would be a nice gesture to invite the Wainwrights. They have entertained me many times."

Sophie felt very adult. Dare she think she and Carlos might announce their engagement?

Since Forester's departure, the atmosphere in the mill had changed. The women sang as they worked and the occasional peal of laughter could be heard over the clanging machines. The men hustled, increasing productivity. Tommy Jones was a much-liked foreman. Quite comfortable with Mr. Jones' leadership, Alberto was considering a trip to Italy.

* * *

Sophie felt the barometer plunge, the atmosphere changed so suddenly she thought a winter storm was coming. Looking up from the ledger, she shivered as Monsieur Dubois walked past her desk and into her father's office.

The glass panes around Alberto's office prevented Sophie from hearing the conversation. She didn't need to hear the words, the fear in her father's eyes told all. The Frenchman had his back to her but the auras emanating from this man were evil. A cackle of laughter cracked through the wall. She watched her father's face fill with darkness, and the room fell silent. Monsieur Dubois stood up, nodded, and turned, a nasty smirk on his face. As he opened the door, he said "Your brother, like mine, is a weakling, but I see I've met my match with you, Mr. Romano. Good day."

Sophie stared at her father as he crumpled into his chair with his hand cupped over his eyes. She ran into the office and threw her arms around him. "Papa, what is wrong!"

Alberto touched Sophie's cheek. "Monsieur Dubois brought some disturbing news about your uncle and the silk farm. Your uncle borrowed a lot of money from known gangsters who now want their money back. Monsieur Dubois has offered to buy Roberto's half of the farm so he can pay his debts. I don't believe him. Roberto is a fool and no businessman, but he wouldn't betray me. Dubois threatened to put me out of business if I don't sell my half of the farm." Alberto laughed. "Idle threats, I can't see Henry Poole & Co doing business with Dubois. I need to be careful about who I trust. Our suspicions about Forester were well founded. Sid Forester also known as Dubois is Monsieur Dubois' younger brother. The black sheep of the family."

Sophie remained silent, afraid to verbalize her thoughts because she had no doubt that the man her uncle had become would betray his brother.

"I shouldn't burden my little girl with business problems." Alberto smiled.

"Father, I'm not a little girl, even if I do call you Papa sometimes." Sophie smiled love into his eyes. "I understand business more than you think. And I think you should go to Italy, Uncle Roberto is in trouble."

"I like being called Papa, it makes me think you still need me. But I agree, Father is appropriate in the office and you are grown up." Alberto sighed.

"Will you go to Italy?"

"I asked Carlos to make a surprise visit to the farm after he has met with Signor Matteo. I expect to hear from him any day."

* * *

Sophie and Alberto left the mill early that day, both tired from the ordeal. A letter sent special messenger from Bologna sat on the silver tray in the hall. Dalton greeted them at the door. Taking Alberto's coat and hat he said, "This arrived about an hour ago. It is marked urgent, sir."

Alberto took the envelope and walked into his study, Sophie on his heels. Sitting behind his mahogany desk he picked up a silver letter opener and glanced at Sophie. "It's from Carlos."

"Read it, Father."

Alberto scanned the letter, took a breath and began:

Dear Mr. Romano,

I hope you are keeping well and the mill is doing well under Tommy Jones, I have faith in that young man. The news from Bologna is not good. Signor Matteo and I met and discussed the recent actions regarding the silk. He has indeed signed a contract with the Lyon Mill, through our friend Dubois. Signor Matteo is quite remorseful, much preferring to keep his business with the Romanos. He told me that Dubois had confirmed his own concerns about the silk and that it had become increasingly difficult to do business with Roberto, although he was reluctant to

*give me specific reasons. Dubois offered him a contract he
couldn't refuse. I'm convinced that Dubois is behind the
troubles at the farm. Sophie and I are certain we saw him
talking to Roberto on several occasions. We also suspected
that the mob might be involved.*

*I am afraid I was not able to secure an order from
Bologna. I think you need to be here. I will wait here a
few more days. If you are not here by the end of the week
I will go to Lucca alone and try to resolve the issues at the
farm. I have arranged to meet with Signor Matteo on my
return to Bologna. It is imperative that you come to Italy.*

"Carlos is right. Dubois has been conniving all along to put us
out of business, both here in England and on the farm in Lucca.
What do you think, Sophie?"

"I think Dubois would do whatever was needed to get what
he wants. Uncle Roberto is mixed up with some bad people
and he's in big trouble."

Alberto put the letter on his desk. "Why didn't Carlos go to
Lucca as I asked?"

"He's waiting for you." Sophie picked up the letter and read
the very end. *How is Sophie?* She was relieved that he had at
least asked after her. She would have preferred "give her my
affections" but she supposed he couldn't say that in a business
letter.

"Father, you need to leave for Italy immediately. Carlos
is waiting for you because Uncle Roberto has no respect for
him. He cannot solve this." Remembering her uncle's temper
and his fight with the thugs, she was afraid for Carlos' safety.
She imagined Roberto as a frightened animal, lashing out at

anything or anyone that threatened him.

"Carlos is doing everything he can. I have faith in his business skills." Alberto frowned. "But I don't understand why he didn't go straight to Lucca as I asked. He knows I am needed at the mill."

Sophie had such a feeling of dread; a terrible accident, fire, even death, flashed before her eyes. She almost fainted. "Father, please, you have to leave, get away from here. I think Carlos is in danger."

"Sophie, take a breath. You look as though you might faint." Alberto stretched his arm across the desk to touch her. "The past few days have been too much for you. You are imagining things. Monsieur Dubois will never carry out his threats. Even the inspector thinks they are idle intimidation. If it makes you feel better, I will review the events of the last few days and decide when I should go to Italy."

She nodded and tried a smile but her insides were so knotted she held her breath against the fear she felt in her stomach. Why didn't her father see the danger?

Letters from Carlos

The next morning Sophie ate breakfast alone. Dalton gave her a message, "Your father asked me to tell you that he is speaking with Mr. Young and Mr. Jones this morning and he will make his decision before dinner tonight. And I thought you might like to know, experience tells me I will need to prepare a travelling bag."

"Oh Dalton, that is such good news." She frowned. "How do you know these things before we know?"

Dalton smiled. "Years of experience and it's my job to know these things, Miss Sophie." He held up the coffee pot. "Coffee?"

The china cup clinked on the saucer as Sophie walked to the window, staring over the lawn to the River Derwent and across to the Romano Silk Mill. A doe stood by the river, not an unusual sight on the lawn of Oak House. Sophie felt its skittishness as it flipped its white tail, sensing danger. Her eyes followed the elegant leaps as the doe moved to safety. And there was the danger: two men appeared from behind an oak tree, pulling a small boat into the river under the willow tree. A shudder of fear rippled down her spine, gripping and twisting around each vertebra; she recognized the taller of the two men—Sid Forester.

The cup flew out of her hand, spilling coffee on the polished floor. She turned to see Dalton in the doorway. "I'm sorry Dalton. You startled me."

"No damage done, I'll send the maid to clean it up."

"Who are those men on the river bank?"

"Where?" Dalton asked, standing beside her.

Sophie looked again, she blinked, both the boat and the men had disappeared. "I know what I saw. Where did they go?"

"Fishermen perhaps. Your father allows the locals to fish on that bank."

"I'm experiencing terrible premonitions of disaster. No one believes me." She looked at Dalton pleadingly, begging him to acknowledge her fears.

"I believe you, Miss Sophie. Your father is a good man. He will resolve the issues. There is no need to worry."

"Thank you. I sense such danger for Carlos. Father has sent him to Uncle Roberto's farm. When I close my eyes, I see violence and fire. There is no detail, but it is real. I can't get the image out of my head."

Dalton held out a letter. "Perhaps this will help."

"It's from Carlos." Dalton nodded as butlers do and left her to read her letter.

Dear Sophie,

    I hope you are keeping well. I had a pleasant journey here. I wish I could say my visit with Signor Matteo was successful. Perhaps your father has told you of my findings.

I met my father in London en route to Italy. He asked me to call on a friend here in Bologna and I am spending a few days with the family before I travel to Lucca. I am enjoying the rest and not looking forward to confronting Roberto. I was hoping your father would join me. I can wait a couple more days. I am not sure when I will have chance to write again or when I'll be home.

Look after yourself, dear Sophie.

Carlos

Sophie read the letter over, her excitement tempered by the coolness of his words. She understood he could say little in her father's letter but this was personal. The lack of any form of endearment or mention that he missed her seemed odd. Were they not engaged? Who were these friends of his father's? And in all the time she had known him he hardly ever mentioned his father, except to say that he did not approve of Carlos' choice to learn sericulture. She felt a tug at her heart. Had Carlos abandoned her and returned to his father? At least, she thought, he is safe in Bologna. She hoped Dalton was right and her father had decided to go to Italy. She would tell him of the letter and he could meet Carlos at these friends' home and they could leave for Lucca together. Satisfied with her own explanations, she went to meet Cook and discuss the menus. She hated to admit it, but she was enjoying being the lady of the house, Cook and Mrs. Simpson were great teachers.

* * *

The last day of the month was a busy time for Sophie in the office. All the invoices had to be completed and checked before being posted. She waved to her father who was speaking with Tommy Jones and Mr. Young. She hoped he was giving them instruction to take over in his absence. When they left he called her into the office.

"Are you going?" Sophie blurted out.

Alberto smiled. "You drive a hard bargain. Yes, I have decided to confront your uncle."

"Will you meet Carlos? He's still in Bologna staying with friends of his father's."

Alberto looked puzzled. "I thought he was already in Lucca."

"I received a letter from him this morning. He's waiting for you. Are you leaving tonight?"

"No, tomorrow night on the night train to London. Sophie, as you learn more about running the mill you will understand how important the workers are to the operation. Mr. Jones just told me O'Reilly approached him for a job. I think you know I fired him for drunkenness. He says he is sober and wants to get his family back. What do you think?"

She thought of the men she had seen earlier that morning. One man was Forester—could the other one have been O'Reilly? About to open her mouth, she quickly decided not say anything, knowing her father would delay his trip if he thought Forester was around. And wasn't Forester in prison? Perhaps she was mistaken. Dalton's explanation of fishermen seemed more plausible.

Alberto didn't wait for an answer. "I think every man deserves a second chance. As long as O'Reilly stays sober on the job, I told Jones to hire him back."

"People should have a second chance," she agreed, but

at the same time she recalled how Forester had defended O'Reilly. Could they be buddies? Convinced that Carlos needed protection, she remained silent.

Alberto's head tipped to one side. "Your words are telling me one thing but your eyes are telling me another. Do you have doubts?"

"Perhaps." She felt guilty for not being honest.

"My father taught me that good workers are a business' most valuable asset. He always maintained that if you treated your workers well they would be loyal and work hard. I want you to remember that. However, I am not blind and I have asked Mr. Jones to keep an eye on O'Reilly. Does that make you feel better?"

"Yes, Father, it does. Now I must get back to work."

* * *

Sophie finished work before Alberto and decided to walk home. She lied to her father, telling him Mr. Young would walk her to the bridge. That was twice today that she had deceived him. She was looking for two men and a rowboat. Walking along the towpath, she realized she hadn't thought this through. At this time of year, the sun set early and the shadows darkened. The path was quiet, the water lapped peacefully against the riverbank, she heard otters scurrying for dinner and frogs plopping from rocks. She smiled, enjoying the purity of nature. The warmth of Oak House beckoned her from across the river. The clouds were closing in and she shivered at the cool of evening. Her shoes slipped on a patch of wet mud and her foot caught in a piece of rope. Steadying herself on a tree branch, she looked up and there it was, the rowboat, pulled partly onto

113

the riverbank. Her heart hammered in her chest, the boat was empty of people but a large tattered tarpaulin covered a mound of something. *What is that smell?* she thought, taking a step towards the boat. She leaned over lifting the tarpaulin with one hand; she quickly pinched her nostrils with the other. The stench of rotten fish and something metallic heaved at her stomach. She jumped back, deciding to walk on. Voices drifted toward her. She couldn't see around the river bend, her heart began thumping again, her steps tentative. Should she turn back? The bridge was only a few yards away, turning back would take time and it was already grey with a sunless dusk. The voices grew louder and a shout pierced her ears. "Dan! I got one, 'ere, 'elp me reel it in." Another voice replied, "Cor! Blimey, 'enry 'iggins, Y'u got a big un."

Sophie exhaled long and hard to slow down her heart. She smiled, seeing two men pulling hard on a bent fishing rod, so intent on their catch they didn't see her run towards the bridge.

Dalton greeted her at the door. She always wondered how he knew she was at the door before she got there.

"Good evening, Miss Sophie." He glanced at the mud on her shoes.

"Sorry, I took the towpath home by the river." She took off her shoes and handed them to him. "Please don't tell Father."

"My lips are sealed, Miss Sophie. However, I don't think it is wise for you to walk home alone." She smiled, knowing Dalton was gently scolding her.

Mayhem at the Mill

A lberto returned to the mill after dinner. He had work to finish before he departed for Italy. Sophie went into the drawing room to write a letter to Carlos.

It was one of those pitch black nights when the clouds covered the moon and stars. She saw the headlights of her father's car turn into the mill. A dot of light appeared from the night watchman's lantern. The lights went on at the mill, a beacon in the dark of night. She opened and closed her eyes to clear the now familiar vision of violence and fire before beginning the letter to Carlos.

> *Dear Carlos, I am pleased Father is joining you. I don't trust Uncle Roberto.*

Overwhelmed by fear, she wanted Carlos to know he was in danger. What danger, she didn't know. The coolness of his letter prompted a different kind of fear. Was he pushing her away? Too distressed to ask him, she decided to tell him about the fishermen, thinking of how silly she had been. She wanted to laugh and wondered what kind of fish Henry Higgins had caught. Looking up from the writing desk she saw lights darting around the river bank and another set of headlights arrive at the mill. *Father has a visitor*, she thought. Curious, she threw her coat around her shoulders, opened the French doors and walked towards the river.

The mill lights shone yellow from the office windows and a light streamed from the open door. She recognized her father's tall frame and a smaller man talking as they went inside. Another figure approached the door holding a lantern. Her blood curdled at the sound of her father's voice as it vibrated across the water, "Stop!" followed by a gun shot and ugly laughter. With relief she heard her father yell, "What are you doing? NO!" Followed by a guttural scream as the door closed and then another gunshot. Again, the violent image and fire flashed in her mind. It wasn't Carlos who was in danger—it was her father.

She ran in the house calling for Dalton. "Gunshots at the mill." Panic and desperation took over.

Dalton opened his mouth to speak when the ground shook violently and a vase fell off the table. Deafened by an explosion, they both ran to the drawing room window. Flames were leaping out of the mill, the night sky a bright orange. Sophie screamed, "Father!" Dalton held on to her. Walking into the hall, he picked up the telephone, "Operator, call the fire brigade, there's been an explosion at Romano Mill and the mill is on fire. There are people inside."

Cook came running upstairs. "What in God's name is going on? Plates jumped off the dresser and are smashed on the floor." She stopped at the sight of the fire. Mrs. Simpson, almost falling as she bumped into the halted cook, said "Oh, God help us!"

Sophie began screaming, "Papa, Papa!" She broke free of Dalton's grip and ran out onto the street. Dalton followed, yelling for Cook and Mrs. Simpson "Gather linen and blankets." The fire engine bell clanged as it passed them on the street, followed by a police wagon. Dalton caught up with Sophie at the bridge. He reached out to stop her going any further. She shook herself free, running towards the mill door. She felt the heat, an inferno, and she tried to get her breath but her lungs wrenched at the smoke and heat. A fireman caught her. "Miss, you can't go in, step back please." Sophie ignored him and tried to shake him off. "NO! Papa! Save him please."

Dalton reached the scene and the fireman said, "Take care of her while we do our job." Dalton nodded and put his arms around Sophie saying, "The fireman will do what they can."

The hoses were already in the river pumping water into the now broken windows. The flames sizzled as the water touched them; leaping higher into the sky, defiantly mocking the firemen's attempts to put them out. Cook and Mrs. Simpson stood next to the bridge holding baskets of useless linens and blankets. No one said it, but they all knew no one could survive such an inferno.

Sophie stared into the flames. The door blew off in one of the smaller explosions. Her eyes tried to penetrate the flames, she willed her father to walk out. Between sobs she whispered, "Papa, don't leave me, please come back."

A crowd gathered on the bridge and a policeman asked them to leave. There was nothing they could do. Sophie refused and Dalton stayed at her side. Taking a blanket, he wrapped it around her. Cook and Mrs. Simpson returned to the house as the crowd dispersed.

* * *

It took the firemen all night to put out the flames and there was little left of the mill but a shell. The wooden looms and silk fed the hungry fire. There was nothing that could have saved the mill.

As dawn broke, Dalton finally managed to get Sophie into the house. Covered in soot, she walked into the kitchen. Mrs. Simpson took her hand, cleaned her up and put her to bed. The doctor had been called to sedate her and she slept for a while.

She woke to see the noon sun high in the sky. She muffled a scream, seeing flames in the bright sun, and the horror of the night came back. Throwing the covers off, she pulled on her robe and walked to the side entrance, down the path and across the lawn, feeling the cool grass on her bare feet, she parted the lazy willow branches and felt their embrace.

The burned out mill glowed in places and black smoke twirled into the blue sky. She sat on the riverbank with her knees tucked under her chin, wondering how the sky could be so blue on a day like today. Tears quietly tumbled down her cheeks. She couldn't believe her father was dead and it was all her fault. The warnings were for her father, not Carlos. "Papa, I'm sorry." More tears streamed and she ached with loneliness and despair as it seeped into her cold, lifeless self. "How will I manage without you? Please, Papa, come back." Staring at the mill she tried to imagine it before the fire; her and Papa walking over the bridge to start the afternoon. The ugly shell invaded her vision; grey-black smoke leaned across the river and twirled around her, suffocating her. She started coughing.

She needed to get away from the evil blackness. She must join her father.

Euphoria filled her mind and she wanted to laugh. "Papa, if you can't come to me, I am coming to you." She slowly walked into the river, embracing the coolness of the water, the sense of freedom as her robe floated on the surface. She'd always liked this robe. It had belonged to her mother and she had found it in the villa. "Mother, I'm coming to be with you and Papa." She felt her long thick hair get heavy with water and then lift to the surface as her neck submerged. The water washed over her open eyes; shadows rippled under the surface. She reached out to touch them. Feeling the warmth of their hands, she slipped away.

* * *

A policeman pounded on the door. Dalton opened it, irritated by the excessive banging. "Miss Romano is drowning," said the distraught constable.

Before Dalton could reply, Mrs. Simpson's voice came from the stairs, "Miss Sophie is not in her bed."

The three ran down the lawn to a commotion on both sides of the riverbank. Another police constable held Sophie in his arms; her robe dripping and her arms lifeless. The solemn group hurried into Oak House.

"She's breathing, just. Call the doctor," the constable said.

"Take her upstairs, I'll get her out of those wet clothes." Mrs. Simpson followed them upstairs.

Dalton called to Cook, "Put some blankets to warm around the fire and bring them up to me."

The doctor arrived, and upon hearing how she was found

floating in the river he took the stairs two at a time. Mrs. Simpson bundled Sophie in warm blankets.

"Mrs. Simpson, you did well. Sophie is suffering from exposure. Fortunately, she was not in the water long enough to drown." He frowned. "She didn't swallow any water and the policeman reported she wasn't struggling, just floating. I'm concerned that she was already unconscious when she fell in the water. She may have hit her head, but I don't see any abrasions. It is possible she doesn't want to wake up. The shock of the fire and death of her father might be too much for her."

"What can we do?" Dalton asked, looking at Mrs. Simpson.

"Mrs. Simpson did the right thing by getting her warm. Keep her warm and don't leave her alone. There is little more I can do. Let her rest tonight. If there is any change, call me immediately."

Sophie slept through the night. In the morning, still groggy, she asked Mrs. Simpson for water. Both Dalton and Mrs. Simpson sighed with relief. Sophie had recovered from her ordeal. Cook made some beef broth to build her strength.

By mid-afternoon Dalton watched beads of perspiration cover her face. Frightened by the sudden change, he called Mrs. Simpson. Sophie's glassy eyes stared into space as Mrs. Simpson rolled her over and changed the soaked sheets. Delirious, Sophie thrashed about the bed, calling, "Papa, Papa, where are you?" She attempted to swing her legs to the floor. "Papa, I'm coming. Wait for me." Dalton gently laid her back down on the bed and tried to sooth her, stroking her tear soaked cheeks. Mrs. Simpson called the doctor.

The doctor placed one hand on her wrist, the other on her forehead. First he looked at Dalton then Mrs. Simpson and slowly shook his head. "Her fever is dangerously high. Keep a cool cloth on her brow and keep her in bed. We have to wait for the fever to break. I need to check in on a patient who suffered a gunshot wound yesterday. I will return in an hour."

"Gunshot wound. That is unusual." Dalton said.

"It is, and what is more unusual, he refuses to say how it happened or call the police. Says it was an accident."

Dalton and Mrs. Simpson took turns at Sophie's bedside. The water ran noisily into the basin as Dalton squeezed the cloth and placed it on Sophie's forehead, moving some long strands of black hair from her eyes. Her breathing was raspy. As she tried to turn, she muttered something incoherent.

"Rest, little Sophie." He felt his heart clamp tight as he considered the prospect of losing her. "Stay with us, Sophie. Use all your strength." He took her limp hand. "I remember the first day you arrived. That little girl leapt into my heart. I offered you strawberry cordial and you gave me such a beautiful smile. I think you were a bit afraid of me at first." He laughed. "By the way, I saw you in the garden imitating my walk. I am a stiff old man at times."

Dalton leaned back in the chair, wondering what would become of them all. He assumed Sophie would go back to Italy, to her uncle. The house would be closed up and he would find another position. He sighed. A shame. He liked working here.

Sophie gave several loud rasping breaths and Dalton jumped out of the chair—afraid he was listening to the death rattle. The thought gave him chills as he remembered his sister dying in his arms. He took another pillow and lifted Sophie's head, sitting her up slightly. She took two more loud breaths and he was thankful when she relaxed. He squeezed another cloth and gently wiped her face. He could feel the heat on his hands. He wished the doctor would come back. He was worried the fever was getting worse.

* * *

The doctor finally returned and followed Mrs. Simpson to Sophie's room. Dalton looked up and said "I think the fever is worse, Doctor."

"I'm afraid that is normal. The doctor felt her forehead, took her temperature and removed her arms from the covers, bathing them with cool water.

"She has stopped moaning and is more settled." Dalton looked at the doctor, hoping this was a good sign.

"Her temperature is extremely high. There is little more we can do but wait." The two men sat back and waited.

"Dalton, wake up." Mrs. Simpson's voice penetrated his sleep. It took him a minute to remember where he was. Daylight shone through a chink in the curtains and the doctor was bending over the bed, blocking his view of Sophie.

"Sophie. How is she?"

"The fever has broken; she's going to be all right." The doctor turned, smiling.

Sophie's recovery was slow, partly because of the fever and partly because of her grief.

Funeral of the Accused

Sophie's pale, gaunt face stared vacantly at the chief inspector. She didn't want to answer questions. She wanted everyone to go away. His voice droned on and on, tears spilled down her face as he asked her about her father. He stood up from the chair at the side of her bed and walked towards the door saying, "We think your father murdered Monsieur Dubois."

Sophie sat bolt upright and screamed, "NEVER! My father would never kill another person. How dare you accuse him of such a thing."

The bedroom door banged against the wall as Dalton burst in. "Leave now! You're upsetting her. I told you it was too soon to question her." Dalton took the chief inspector by the arm and walked him out of the house.

Sophie was stunned to hear Dalton raise his voice. It felt good to know someone was protecting her. She'd always seen kindness in his eyes. Taking a few deep breaths, she realized that she felt better and, for the first time since the fire, not only did she feel alive but she wanted to live.

Mrs. Simpson arrived with a tray but Sophie was already out of bed. "Mrs. Simpson, please take the tray to the drawing room."

"Oh Miss Sophie, I am so happy to see you up."

Mrs. Simpson escorted a rather shaky Sophie down the stairs and into the drawing room. The black dress Mrs. Simpson insisted she wear drained even the paleness from her face.

"Dalton, open the curtains. My father would not want such doom and gloom." She gasped as the curtains parted and revealed the ruins across the river. She looked away; her inner dialogue telling her to be strong for her father.

"It's good to see you up and about, Miss Sophie," Dalton said.

"The chief inspector accused my father of murder. What is that about?"

Dalton hesitated, not sure if she was ready to hear the details.

"I need to know. Please tell me what you know."

"May I?" Dalton said pointing to the chair. She nodded.

"Just before the explosion there were gunshots, some witnesses said they heard one, others said they heard two or three."

"There were two shots." Sophie said with certainty. "After the first shot, I heard my father shout 'no' and then a second shot. That's when I came in to fetch you. My father was being shot at, not doing the shooting."

"The police say not, Miss Sophie. The police found the remains of two badly burned bodies in the mill. One was your father and the other one was Monsieur Dubois with a bullet in his head. There were no signs of anyone else except the night watchman and he was found unconscious on the river bank. The police think the blast threw him away from the building and, other than temporary deafness from the blast and memory loss from a bump on the head, he was unhurt. He won't make a credible witness.

"I need to speak with the chief inspector. There were other people near the mill that night. I saw lights from lanterns and car headlights. Father didn't say he was meeting anyone. He went to finish off his work before leaving for Italy. What was Monsieur Dubois doing at the mill?"

"Are you sure you are well enough, Miss Sophie? The chief inspector can be harsh. He is convinced the evidence will prove your father's guilt. He had motive and opportunity."

"My father's name must be cleared. Do you believe he is a murderer?"

"No, Miss Sophie, I don't."

"That Frenchman was threatening my father's business here in Derby, the farm in Lucca and his customer in Bologna. My father had motive and the more the police investigate, the more motive they will find. We have to find someone who had an even bigger motive. My father did not kill Monsieur Dubois."

As if on cue, pounding came from the front door. "The chief inspector. Why he cannot ring the bell like a civilized person, I do not know." It was unusual for Dalton to break protocol and speak in such a familiar way.

"Good afternoon, Miss Romano. I see you are recovering from your ordeal. Please accept my condolences."

"Thank you. My father did not murder the Frenchman. There were other people near the mill that night."

"The evidence says otherwise. Your father's exact words to me were 'I'll make sure he is reckoned with' and now Monsieur Dubois is dead."

"Father didn't mean he would kill him. Chief Inspector, he is not a murderer."

"Miss Romano, tell me what you thought you saw?"

"Chief Inspector, I know what I saw."

She watched the chief's face closely as she told him about the lights and the shots and her father's voice and in what order they came. She suggested the night watchman heard and saw the goings on.

The inspector retorted, "The night watchman has no memory of the events. Who were these people at the mill. I need names to follow up on."

"I don't know. I was too far away to see. However, the day before the fire, I saw two fishermen and a rowboat on the riverbank. Perhaps they saw something. One of the fishermen called his friend Henry Higgins and the other name may have been Dan. They are local people and easy to find."

"I need evidence. What did you see that night?"

"It was dark. I recognized no one. I assumed one lantern belonged to the night watchman, the others I don't know. A second vehicle drove up after my father arrived and I saw the silhouette of my father and a shorter man in the light from the door."

"And where were you to see all this?"

"I was sitting at the desk over there by the window. When I saw the lights, I walked down to the riverbank. My father's voice, shouted 'Stop' and then there was a gunshot and then he said, 'What are you doing? No'. I ran inside to call Dalton and then the mill exploded. Inspector, my father was not the shooter. He was being shot at. He went to the mill to do some work and he had no plans to meet anyone.

"The evidence suggests he was the shooter. A gun was found on the floor. I concede, it could have been in self defense and my report will reflect that."

"My father didn't own a gun. It wasn't his. Ask Dalton."

His feet shuffled slightly and he continually cleared his throat. "Your father never owned a gun?"

"No, never!"

"Something is not adding up. I am convinced the fire was arson, not a convenient accident. Before I close the file, I'll speak to those fishermen. I suspect the night watchman knows more than he is saying and the memory loss may be temporary. He might have been threatened."

She stared defiantly at the inspector and repeated, "My father did not kill Monsieur Dubois. He did not own a gun. I will not rest until I have cleared his name." Sophie pulled the bell for Dalton. "Please show the chief inspector out. We are finished here. Good day, Chief Inspector."

* * *

The rain fell hard on the window, waking Sophie to a sad day. Today was Papa's funeral. She parted the curtains but could see little as the pouring rain ran in rivulets down the windowpane. She wondered why it always rained for funerals. Her father would have preferred sunshine. Just thinking about him stabbed painfully at her heart. She glanced at the black dress Mrs. Simpson had hung outside her wardrobe. She hated black. She remembered wearing a black dress on the day of her mother's funeral. Thankfully, her father didn't believe in the traditional Victorian mourning and had allowed her to wear ordinary clothes after the funeral. The undertaker had been quite offended when Sophie announced she would not be mourning beyond the funeral. He had tried to sell her a locket for a lock of her father's hair or a mourning brooch. It all seemed macabre. Not able to cope while she was ill, she had left most of the arrangements to Dalton and Mrs. Simpson, which turned out to be more elaborate than either she or her father would have liked.

Seeing her father's coffin through the glass of the hearse, she felt her knees give way. Dalton caught her arm and helped her into the carriage behind the hearse. The horses began to move and she heard the clop-clop of the hooves and felt the carriage sway.

Loneliness engulfed her. Her heart was breaking. A gentle voice said, "Don't be sad, Sophie. We love you." Both her mother and father sat in the seat opposite. She reached across and found only emptiness at first; then she smelt the sweet scent of her mother's lavender, and felt the coarseness of her father's hand brush her own. It felt warm and cold all at the same time. "Leave the mill and start a new and different life." The carriage stopped. "Papa, Mama," she called but they were gone.

Sophie remembered little about the ceremony, except the swarm of sombre people in black, buzzing like summer flies. Mrs. Simpson said she had fainted and the doctor ordered her to lie down. She lay on her bed until the noise abated. Pleased it was over, she went into her father's study, feeling his presence, his manly odour of cigars and whiskey. Curling her legs underneath her, she snuggled into his burgundy wingback chair and, feeling his warm embrace, she slept.

The dusky light of morning flooded the room as Mrs. Simpson pulled back the curtains. She stretched from sleep and a wool blanket fell to the floor. "Mrs. Simpson, what time is it?"

"Seven-thirty. Did you sleep?"

"Why am I in Father's study?"

"You fell asleep in his chair. You looked so peaceful, so I covered you with a blanket and let you sleep. How are you?"

"Rested. I'll go and change."

"Shall I bring a tray up?"

"No, I'll have coffee in the drawing room. I want to write to Carlos and my uncle. I expect there are other people I need to notify." She thought about Carlos and wondered why there had been no letter from him. It surprised her to realize that only five days had passed since the fire, hardly time for a letter to reach Italy. She wondered if anyone had telegraphed.

Anchored at her father's desk, she touched the things that he had touched only a few days before. The ornate silver letter opener lay across an opened envelope and she wondered if he had read its contents, or if he had been disturbed. She picked the letter up and pressed it to her cheek, hoping to somehow feel him. She sniffed the envelope and frowned—it smelt of paraffin. She pulled the letter out of the envelope. It was smudged with dirty finger marks. A child-like scroll read *Meet me at the Mill at 8 o'clock. Monsieur Dubois will greet you.* There was no signature. Her heart began to race, was this proof that her father had been lured to the mill that night? She was convinced the paraffin smell was proof that the person who wrote the letter also set the fire. Who had written the note? The handwriting looked vaguely familiar.

The drawing room was brighter than the study—offensively bright. The morning sun seemed to illuminate the mill ruins. She squinted, pulled the chair to the desk and picked up the pen. The words from the note kept spinning in her head, making it impossible to write letters. Strange random half thoughts of loneliness, conflict and fear bombarded her mind. She wanted to search her father's papers to compare the note's handwriting, before showing it to the chief inspector.

The slight squeak of the drawing room floor made her aware that Dalton had entered. Sophie continued her jumbled thoughts, staring at the ruined mill, and without turning she said, "I can't believe he has gone. Dalton, what is to become of me?"

"Miss Sophie, Mr. Fotheringham, your father's solicitor, is here to see you. Perhaps his advice and your father's wishes will help answer your questions."

"Yes, thank you, Dalton."

A robust, immaculately dressed man in his fifties walked into the drawing room.

"Good afternoon, Miss Romano. Please accept my condolences." His arms tight to his side he appeared to flip his hands. Sophie wanted to giggle at this penguin-like man.

"Thank you."

"Your father has willed all of his estate to you. That includes the mill, the villa in Lucca and half of the silk farm. There are no other bequests. You are the sole beneficiary." Mr. Fotheringham looked around the room. "There is no mention of the family residence."

"Our family residence is the villa in Lucca. Father leased this house and most of the furniture belongs to the landlord. At the time, he was not sure we would stay in Derby. I think he always intended to buy it but never got around to it."

"Miss Romano, because you are a minor all the assets are held in trust until you turn twenty-one. You will receive an allowance based on your father's assets." He shuffled some papers, cleared his throat, looking extremely uncomfortable. "Miss Romano, there is no easy way to say this. I'm sorry to inform you that your father depleted most of his liquid assets to pay the debt on the farm in Lucca. The assets are limited to the mill, which is heavily mortgaged and currently in ruins. The mill was insured with Lloyds of London. I doubt there are enough funds to rebuild and the bank will insist that Lloyds pay off the mortgage first. If the police deem the fire to be arson, Lloyds will not pay." Mr. Fotheringham's face creased with anguish. Even this calculating solicitor appeared touched by the tragedy and was obviously trying to find words to ease the bad news. "I am truly sorry, Miss Romano. It is unlikely there will be enough money for an allowance. I have written to your father's brother. As the closest relative, he is your guardian. Arrangements will be made for you to travel to Italy."

"I refuse to go to Italy. My uncle is not my guardian." Sophie didn't know what else to say. The thought of Aunt Maria getting her own way and adopting her filled her with dread, although the idea of living in the villa with her mother's spirit, and she was certain her father would be there too, was tempting.

"There is no alternative. I have to follow the law and your father made no provision for guardianship."

"He would not want me to go to Aunt Maria and Uncle Roberto. That was an oversight." It suddenly occurred to Sophie that her uncle had not attended the funeral. Uncle Roberto had changed over the years, but not his love for his brother. "Mr. Fotheringham, did anyone notify my uncle of father's death?"

"My office sent a cable the day of the disaster. We did not receive a reply. I thought he might come to the funeral."

Sophie blinked back tears. Had Uncle Roberto changed so drastically that he no longer loved his brother? "Perhaps you now understand why I cannot go to Italy. I am quite capable of looking after myself."

Mr. Fotheringham sighed and placating Sophie with a tap on her hand he said, "There, there, I understand this has all been a terrible shock. You cannot stay here; with no funds to pay the lease, the landlord will insist you vacate the property. The staff, have been given notice. Dalton has agreed to stay with you until the end of the month. As soon as I hear from your uncle, we will make arrangements for you to leave."

Leave, she thought, no I can't leave. "What if I found work?"

"Sorry. You are a minor and need a guardian."

"Marriage. What if I were to marry? I am engaged to Carlos Wainwright. He is currently in Italy on business."

"If your uncle approves, yes, you can marry and then you would be your husband's responsibility."

Italy – The Silk Farm in Ruins

T he postman waved a letter at Sophie from the path as he approached the front door. She ran to greet him.

"A letter from Italy, Miss. I see your face light up when I deliver these letters." The postman gave her a wink.

"Thank you. It's from my fiancé."

Sophie ripped the envelope open, almost tearing the letter. Three pages long, her heart filled with love, Carlos would rescue her. They would get married.

> *Dear Sophie*
>
> *I hope you are well. I waited for your father in Bologna. When he didn't arrive, I took the train to Lucca. Signor Matteo had indicated there was trouble at the farm. I left a message for your father, so I assume he will be here tomorrow, which will not be too soon. I arrived in Lucca this morning and what a terrible sight greeted me. The farm is in ruins and Roberto and Maria are nowhere to*

be found. The silkworms are mostly dead, the warehouse is empty, the farmhouse has been ransacked.

I am happy to say the villa has not been touched and is in one piece, I'm writing this from the kitchen table, which has fond memories. The old truck is still here, so Roberto and Maria can't be far away. The telephone isn't working so I drove into Lucca to report this to the police. I can't say the police were helpful. They seemed to think Roberto was mixed up in something illegal. He had been keeping company with some known thugs. However, they agreed to send someone here tomorrow. I called my father's friends in Bologna but your father has not arrived, nor has he left a message. After the police leave tomorrow, I am returning to Bologna. I can only wait another day. I have to meet my father. When your father arrives, I regret to say that I have decided to join my father's export business. I liked the silk business, but the events in Lucca and the uncertainty in Derby have convinced me there is no future for me at Romano Silk Mill. I am staying in Italy, working out of my father's office in Bologna. My parents do not approve of our engagement, they say you are too young at sixteen, and I agree.

Please don't be too sad. You and your father work well together and in spite of the farm in ruins, you still have the mill in Derby and when you are older you will find a husband worthy of you. Good bye my dearest Sophie, I will always remember you and perhaps one day we will meet again.

Tears were dripping on the page, smearing the words and she

brushed her eyes to read the last line. Standing by the open door, copious, unashamed tears flowed down her cheeks and dripped on to her blouse. Dalton appeared at her side and closed the door: his arm gently guiding her into the drawing room.

"Whatever is it, Miss Sophie?"

"Carlos isn't coming back." Tears flowing but her voice quite calm she added, "The farm in Lucca is in ruins." She gave a high-pitched hysterical laugh. "And my guardians, Uncle Roberto and Aunt Maria, have run away. I have no one, which is preferable to those two."

"You have me, Miss Sophie. I will not abandon you."

"But Dalton, the solicitor said he had let all the staff go. There is no money to pay you. I'm to be sent to Italy but," she handed Carlos' letter to Dalton, "my aunt and uncle have disappeared."

Dalton read the letter, raising his eyebrows. "I'm not sure what this means. Rest assured, I will stay with you until the solicitor makes arrangements for your care." She saw the concern in Dalton. He really does care about me, she thought.

"Why do you care?"

"It's a long story. I had a niece, my elder sister's daughter. You remind me of her, full of high spirits and fun. She ran off when my sister died. She was sixteen, the same age as you. She felt lonely and abandoned and I should have done more for her, but I couldn't find her. I haven't seen her in seven years. I don't know what happened to her."

Sophie felt chilled, her wet, tear-soaked blouse cold against her skin. But Dalton's words were warm and comforting. She stopped crying.

Cook left two days later, one of the neighbours having hired her. Mrs. Simpson left in tears the next day. She took a position

135

with a duke and duchess near Manchester; her tears hardly masking her pride. Mrs. Simpson had always been good to Sophie and her family, but Sophie sensed she had thought them beneath her. A position in a duke's household was a big step up.

* * *

Stillness and emptiness filled Sophie's days. She sat at the writing desk in the drawing room. The room looked the same, but the sounds were different, because there were no sounds. She missed Mrs. Simpson bustling upstairs with clean linen or Cook humming as she baked, and most all her, father's voice from the study or his footsteps as he approached the drawing room. Dalton's footsteps echoed in the empty house. Her pen was stiff, as though resisting writing. She decided to visit Carlos' parents. She wondered if he would change his mind when he heard about the mill and her father. She knew it was unrealistic, as he had to have known by now what had happened and he had not even written in condolence. She risked her heart breaking again. *I have to try*, she thought.

At first Dalton refused to drive her. "Miss Sophie, the Wainwrights didn't even attend your father's funeral and Carlos has made it clear how he feels. This is not a good idea."

"If you won't drive me, I will walk."

Dalton agreed, and they drove across town to the Wainwright mansion. Letter in hand, Sophie took a deep breath. She was dressed appropriately in a dark grey suit and a black and grey hat, to indicate she was in mourning. The butler greeted her at the door. "I would like to see Mrs. Wainwright please."

The butler bowed. "I'll see if Mrs. Wainwright is home." He

136

opened the door for her to walk in, indicating she should stay in the hall.

Mrs. Wainwright appeared from what she assumed was the drawing room. "Miss Romano, how nice to see you. Please accept my condolences. Such a tragedy."

"Thank you, Mrs. Wainwright. I had a disturbing letter from Carlos. I would like to contact him."

"Carlos is working with his father. He tells us the Romano Mill and farm are in ruins."

"I don't think he knows about the mill here or the death of my father. I am sure I would have heard from him." Sophie was uncomfortable having this conversation in the hall but it was obvious she was not going to be invited into the drawing room. "We are engaged to be married. Carlos made me a promise when we were in Italy this summer." She felt her cheeks go scarlet and Mrs. Wainwright's ample bosom heaved up and down as she controlled her breathing. "I don't understand why I haven't heard from him since the fire and my father's death."

"Your summer romance was nothing more than a schoolgirl's crush and my son had his fling. He doesn't want to see you anymore. Your family is in ruins." She fidgeted with her hands, hesitating before adding. "Mr. Wainwright and I could not allow such a marriage and, at sixteen, you are far too young to marry. I am sorry for your loss. Please leave now."

Sophie pushed the letter in her hand. "Please give him this." Mrs. Wainwright glanced at the letter and to Sophie's surprise she took it. Sophie saw a brief hint of sympathy cross her face. Mrs. Wainwright nodded towards the butler who bowed and opened the door.

Beyond crying, Sophie stomped to the automobile. Dalton stood beside the open car door, which gave Sophie a sense of worth, knowing Mrs. Wainwright was watching her.

"You were right, Dalton. I shouldn't have come. Carlos was having a summer fling, nothing more." Even as she said the words, she knew it wasn't true, but she also knew she could not fight the Wainwrights. Carlos had loved her during the summer. Perhaps his promise of marriage had been unrealistic, but she had no doubt that he was being manipulated by his parents.

* * *

Chaos greeted them back at Oak House. A variety of vehicles were lined up in front of the house, including a truck and a police wagon. Mr. Fotheringham was standing on the doorstep speaking with the chief inspector and two policemen. Three burly workmen were leaning on a truck, arms folded defiantly. Dalton parked and jumped out. "What is going on here?"

Mr. Fotheringham spoke first. "I need to speak with Miss Romano. I have distressing news."

Dalton's gaze went from Fotheringham to the inspector to the men. "Why are you here?" Dalton directed his question to the inspector.

"Mr. Fotheringham arrived to find these men trying to break into the house and alerted the police."

Sophie stared at the men near the truck. Hesitating, she stepped out of the auto. She recognized O'Reilly as he limped towards her. Sophie's heart clenched and her stomach flipped to the point of nausea at the sour odour of his alcohol breath. The scene before her began to move, people and vehicles spinning out of control. She was falling into a deep dark hole and it felt good to escape, until something assaulted her nostrils.

She opened her eyes, lying on the sofa, surrounded by people.

"Miss Sophie, you fainted. Can you sit up?" Dalton handed her a glass of brandy. "Drink this. You'll feel better." The combination of smelling salts and brandy jolted her to life. "Mr. Fotheringham and the inspector need to speak with you. I will make some tea and be right back." He gave her a reassuring smile.

Sophie sat up and sipped on the brandy. She didn't like the taste or the burn as it passed her throat, but she liked the warmth it gave her insides. "When is someone going to tell me what is going on? Who are those men?" She directed her question to the inspector.

"The debt collector sent those men. I'm sorry to say your father owed a lot of money in town. They want to be paid and the workers are owed a week's wages."

"I have no money."

"Unfortunately, they will take whatever you have: jewellery, furniture, anything."

Sophie frowned. "Can they do that? Just break into the house."

"No. It is fortuitous that Mr. Fotheringham happened to come by and fetched the police. I have stopped them for now but they do need payment. Mr. Fotheringham will explain the legalities."

"Inspector, you do know that one of those men, O'Reilly, was involved in the mill fire and my father's death."

"Miss, we questioned him. He was a person of interest and he is a known associate of Sid Forrester, who we now know is Sid Dubois. Both had grievances. Motive to attack the mill and your father. Forester known as Dubois was in jail at the time of the fire and murder and O'Reilly has a solid alibi." He looked sympathetically at Sophie. "I'm sorry. The evidence points to your father."

Dalton arrived with a tray of tea. "Perhaps, Inspector, you are not aware that Mr. O'Reilly received a bullet wound on the night of the fire."

The inspector swung around, challenging Dalton. "He wasn't in town that night. His wife confirmed she'd thrown him out and he stayed at his brother's in Macclesfield. Why did you not come forward with this information before? Where did it come from?"

"I didn't give it much thought. When Miss Sophie was ill with fever the day after the fire, the doctor stayed at her bedside most of the night. He left for a short while to attend to a patient with a gunshot wound. He mentioned he had been trying to persuade the patient to go to the police. He couldn't understand why he refused to report the incident. I think we know why. The doctor never mentioned him by name, but it was common knowledge that Patrick O'Reilly had sustained a gunshot wound and the only incident involving guns that I know of happened the night of the fire. I doubt his wife threw him out. He was at home hiding."

"I noticed he was limping. This happened the night of the fire? I will speak with the doctor."

"And the letter I found on father's desk."

"Miss Romano, what letter?"

Sophie picked up the letter from her father's desk. She brought it to her face and sniffed. "I can smell paraffin." She handed it to the inspector, who took it from her with a handkerchief and sniffed.

"Um, I can smell paraffin among other things." He screwed up his nose. "It looks as though we have some good finger marks."

He moved his head to one side. "This is valuable information."

The inspector left, promising to remove the men from the premises.

All is Gone

Mr. Fotheringham cleared his throat. "Miss Romano, what you saw today were men hoping to grab whatever they could before the bank. The bank will auction off the contents of the house." He stopped, as Dalton came back in the room.

Sophie said, "I would like Dalton to stay."

"The auction has been booked for the day after tomorrow. The auctioneer is a reputable man, but his job is to be ruthless and acquire as much as he can for the bank. I suggest you pack a trunk of your personal belongings and anything precious to you and remove it from the house."

"Perhaps Cook could take care of my trunk for a while. She works at the neighbours now."

"Ideal. Be careful, those men are watching the house. I don't trust what they might do if they see you moving anything."

"I asked the inspector to post a constable outside the house." Dalton smiled at Sophie.

The room fell silent and Mr. Fotheringham fidgeted with

papers from his leather case. Sophie stared into nothing, thinking of her mother's precious ornaments. She touched a figurine on the side table, Italian made. She had never really thought about the furnishings or trinkets that adorned the house. Parting with them was like parting with her parents. This was home. The china ornaments, glass vases, and trinkets were her mother and the cigars, glass decanters filled with golden liquid, bookcases full of books in his study, were her father. Burning tears boiled hot onto her cheeks as she imagined strangers grabbing at the family's possessions and obliterating her memories. How would she survive without them? Dalton sat beside her and handed her his handkerchief. He placed his arm around her shoulders, a little awkwardly. he wasn't used to such familiarity.

"If that is all, Mr. Fotheringham. I think Miss Sophie needs to rest."

"Um, well actually," Mr. Fotheringham cleared his throat vigorously. She had begun to understand this was a nervous habit and she held Dalton's free hand. "I have received some disturbing news from Italy." He looked at Dalton. "Could I have a brandy please?" Dalton patted Sophie's hand and poured them all a brandy before returning to his seat.

Mr. Fotheringham took a big gulp. "As I said, I received some disturbing news from Italy. Miss Romano, it seems your uncle was forced to sell his share of the farm. The police are not certain but the evidence indicates that your uncle was heavily in debt to some unsavoury characters associated with criminal activity. He went mad and proceeded to wreck the farm and destroy the silkworms." He cleared his throat again, sipping more brandy. "In retaliation, the gangster—the police suspect organized crime—murdered your aunt and uncle. Their bodies were found a week ago in a storage shed near the mulberry grove. The police think they had been dead a few days."

Sophie felt her stomach twist as she imagined the scene. The shed was where Uncle Roberto kept the pruning shears, spades and soil nutrients for the mulberry trees. She hated the odour in that shed. She felt her stomach wrench again, thinking of the added stench of bodies. She and Carlos had often met behind the shed, an ideal trysting place hidden from the house and farm. Carlos must have been there immediately after the attack and not known they were dead. The police, as corrupt as the gangsters, had probably been bribed to ignore Carlos. It also explained Uncle Roberto's absence from the funeral. As much as she disliked Uncle Roberto and Aunt Maria, they did not deserve such a tragic end.

Mr. Fotheringham handed Sophie some papers. "Your father gave me this to keep in my safe. It is the legal title to the villa in Lucca. It is in your name only and, as a result, not part of the farm. He told me if anything happened to him, you would always have the villa."

"That's the best news you've given me all day. I probably will never go back to Lucca but I am happy in the knowledge that no one else can take it. My parents are at peace in the villa."

Mr. Fotheringham frowned, puzzled by her comment. "Once things settle down you could sell it."

"No, I won't ever sell it."

"You might want to reconsider. It is a valuable property. The proceeds of the sale would provide a modest allowance."

"No!" Sophie stamped her foot. "If it falls into ruin, so be it. I could never let strangers disturb Alberto and Martina Romano's spirits."

Mr. Fotheringham sighed. "As you wish, Miss Romano. I will

continue to take care of your affairs, but you have no guardian."

"My youngest sister lives in Hastings. Miss Sophie can come with me. That's if it is acceptable to you, Miss Sophie."

"I have no one else and nowhere to go. Hastings sounds interesting."

"Please leave me a forwarding address." Mr. Fotheringham placed his papers back into the leather case and walked out.

* * *

In spite of the police presence, Sophie spotted O'Reilly lurking around the property that night. She shuddered. It felt creepy to be watched. Every time she closed her eyes, she saw O'Reilly's angry smirking face coming towards her. She slept fitfully, waking in horror from a nightmare of Uncle Roberto chasing her with monstrous silkworms and Dalton chasing O'Reilly. She was running but they were catching up. She sat up in bed with beads of perspiration running down her back and gulping for air. She swung her legs to the floor and crept to the window, tentatively parting the silk curtains. The garden and street were empty. She sighed with relief, thinking O'Reilly must have gone home to sleep. She wrapped her robe around her, pleased that she had insisted that Mrs. Simpson clean and dry it after her episode in the river. She felt her mother's arms around her little girl when she wore it. She would pack that first.

Her bedroom was a mess, with clothes everywhere. It was tough deciding what to pack and what to leave. She assumed she would be living a simpler life so it was easy to discard the fancy clothes. Mrs. Simpson had taught her that a lady needed a good wardrobe for visiting and entertaining. She was not comfortable in corsets that pinched waists and popped bosoms or wearing dresses with puffy sleeves and copious skirts. Sophie preferred modest and practical styles. She left all but one gown hanging in the wardrobe. Her fingers slid down the emerald green silk remembering the night Carlos came for dinner. Taking it off its hanger, she carefully folded it.

Dalton brought her steamer trunk up from the cellar. She opened the lid and stared into the empty space, feeling an intense desire to fill it with memories. She ran into her father's study, collecting his pens and ink blotter, some of her favourite books and his cigars. With urgency, she packed them carefully at the bottom of the trunk. She added his silk scarves, they smelled of him as she brushed them against her face.

Choosing things of her mother's was more difficult. Finally, she decided on her silver dressing table set, brush and combs, her perfume spray, jewellery and Italian figurines. She allowed herself two of her favourites; one was a mother and child, another was a small dog. Smiling, she remembered her mother telling her to put it down or it would break. She packed these in her woollen skirts and placed the emerald dress on top and filled the remainder of the trunk with her belongings. She found an ornate tapestry carpetbag in her mother's wardrobe and smiled, remembering her mother clutching it on the train during their journey from Italy. Sophie selected some things she would need on her own journey and placed them in her mother's bag.

It took two of them to bring the trunk downstairs and set it by the door, next to Dalton's Gladstone bag. Familiar with sudden and perhaps many moves, butlers packed light. Sophie thought it sad to have so few belongings.

"How are we going to get my trunk to Cook? O'Reilly is

watching us."

"Miss Sophie, forgive me. I deceived you, knowing the workers might try to steal your trunk. The inspector is waiting outside with the police van. One of his constable's will take it to the train station." Dalton opened the door and the inspector stepped in as two constables lifted Sophie's trunk.

The inspector glanced at Sophie. "The station master has been told the trunk is under police custody and not to let anyone near it. He will put it on the train before you board tomorrow."

"Thank you, Inspector."

"I have some good news, Miss Romano. I have confirmed that O'Reilly was shot at the mill that night. Sid Forester, known as Dubois, was not in jail at the time. There was a mix-up between the British and French authorities. Henry Higgins confirmed he was fishing the day before. He and his mate saw two men answering the description of O'Reilly and Forester row over from the other bank, leaving the boat exactly where you said you saw it. We believe there was a conspiracy. The best evidence we have are the fingerprints on the letter luring your father to the mill that night. They had both O'Reilly's and Forester's finger marks on the letter and envelope. Proof, at the very least, that there was a conspiracy."

"Thank you, Inspector. My father did not kill anyone. Please exonerate him." Sophie was happy the inspector was taking her seriously.

The auctioneer arrived early the next morning. Sophie and Dalton sat at the kitchen table in silence, listening to the hum of people gathering for the auction. Mr. Fotheringham arrived to supervise. Dalton and Sophie left through the servant's entrance as the auctioneer began his jabbering. The sale of the

Romanos' life had begun.

Sophie was an orphan as she walked beside Dalton towards the train station, not sure if she was walking away from life or towards a new one.

* * *

A chill wind tunnelled down the platform and blew around Sophie's skirt as she sat on the bench. She pulled her coat tighter to stop shivering. Dalton put his bag down at the side of the bench and went to get some hot tea. She welcomed the tea, wrapping her fingers around the mug. She jumped when a voice said, "I'm glad I caught you."

"Inspector, you scared me half to death, what is it?" Sophie said, brushing some spilled tea from her coat.

Catching his breath, the inspector continued, "All charges against your father have been dropped. You were right, Miss Romano. Your father did not murder anyone. He was the victim. The mill fire was arson and your father's and Monsieur Dubois' deaths were murder."

Not sure if she had understood, Sophie remained silent, digesting the inspector's words; words she had waited so long to hear.

"The doctor confirmed O'Reilly's gunshot wound and the time it happened. He also disclosed O'Reilly smelled of paraffin and was covered in black smoke the night he was called to treat him."

"I told you my father would never kill anyone. Those men killed him in the fire."

"Sid Forester, alias Dubois, planned the whole thing. He incited O'Reilly with anger towards your father for firing him.

148

That, you already knew. But you might not have known that Sid Forrester Dubois was Monsieur Dubois' younger brother. He was the black sheep of the family, frequently in trouble with the law. However, Monsieur Dubois used his brother to stir up unrest in the mill, to put your father out of business. Although the details are not clear, the Frenchman is connected to some shady people in Italy and is most likely responsible for threatening the farm and for your uncle and aunt's death. "

"I already know. Carlos Wainwright and Mr. Fotheringham told me about the sale and destruction at the farm in Italy. There's nothing left. I still don't understand who shot Monsieur Dubois and how the mill caught fire."

"Remember the note you gave me? Well, we discovered a similar note in Monsieur Dubois' belongings. Unbeknownst to anyone but his brother, Sid was staying at the Railway Hotel. The note requested that he meet your father at the mill that night. Sid Dubois, angry because his brother had used him, conspired with O'Reilly to shoot his brother and when your father tried to stop him, he turned the gun on him. The bullet missed and hit O'Reilly in the thigh, causing him to drop the lantern. Knowing the place had been dowsed in paraffin, they escaped, locking the door behind them. It took only minutes for the silk bales to catch fire and explode. Confident that all the evidence had gone up in smoke, Sid Dubois thought he was in the clear and planned to escape to Europe. When the night watchman's memory returned, he terrified the man with threats. It was the finger marks on the letter and the statement from Henry Higgins that gave us the proof we needed to arrest them. Miss Romano, your father can rest in peace. It is the hangman's noose for those men."

The train let out a blast of steam and the conductor yelled,

"All aboard."

Sophie was so grateful that she had a strong desire to embrace the inspector, but good manners prevented such a show of affection. Instead, she said, "Thank you."

Hastings to Bexhill

The swaying train quickly lulled Sophie to sleep. She felt safe next to Dalton and she realized how insecure she had felt for a long time. They had been silent for most of the first part of the journey. After changing trains in London, both having slept a little, Dalton began to speak.

"Miss Sophie, I haven't spoken of this before. My sister is offering us a roof for a short time but I'm afraid you will need to find work. I have made application for a butler's position in a house near London. If I am hired, I don't expect to be in Hastings long. My sister made enquires about office work for you but nothing paid well enough for you to even rent a room and Doris doesn't have room for you in her house. She has a friend who works at The Sackville Hotel in Bexhill-on-Sea, not far from Hastings. Do you think you could work as a maid? The Sackville is a prestigious and reputable hotel. The wages are modest, but it does include room and board."

"So much has happened, I hadn't given my future any thought. I have to work. Mr. Fotheringham gave me a little money but it won't last long. I am not sure what maids do, but Mrs. Simpson taught me how to clean and how to take care of linen. Cook showed me how to plan food for a dinner party."

Dalton laughed. "I don't think Cook's dinner parties will help you but cleaning and linen will. I am sorry you have been brought down to maid's work instead of running your father's mill."

"Don't be. I loved my father and enjoyed the mill because I could be close to him. I think the dream of me running the mill was more for my father than me. I actually don't miss it. Working as a maid in a hotel sounds exciting." She put her head to one side and said, "I really don't have a choice. Do I?"

"Miss Sophie, you are intelligent and very mature for your age. I don't think the fine life of a lady would have suited you."

"Perhaps not, but I never expected to be a maid either. Please Dalton, call me Sophie. You don't work for my father anymore."

* * *

Doris, Dalton's sister, made them welcome. It was a tight squeeze in their little house. Sophie shared a bed with Doris's two daughters and Dalton slept on the parlour floor. The letter from London arrived two days later and he headed there to take up his new appointment. She was sad to say goodbye. Dalton's kindness had been the thread that had kept her attached to her old life and now it had broken for good. She wondered if she would ever see him again.

* * *

Riding the omnibus to Bexhill-on-Sea to meet Mrs. Banks,

the head housekeeper at The Sackville Hotel, Sophie thought about her life in Italy, missing her mother. She realized she could hardly remember what she looked like, but her voice of encouragement was clear in Sophie's head, as was her father's. She wondered if they had anticipated tragedy. There was no doubt her father had judged Carlos for who he was. *Carlos,* she thought, *what happened?* He had loved her and he was serious when they talked about being engaged. His letter said, 'perhaps we'll meet again.' Unlikely, she thought as the omnibus jerked to a stop. Taking a deep breath, she stepped onto the Promenade. The air was crystal clear, the sky blue and the sea calm, waves gently rolling up the shingle beach. Her past, now a distant memory, had begun to fade from her thoughts.

Sophie knocked on the service door at the back of the hotel. She took a gulp of air and swallowed her nerves, forcing a smile as a kindly man opened the door. "My name is Sophie Romano and I'm here about the..." her eyes searching into the dark, not unpleasant hallway, she continued, "maid's position."

"You're 'ere to see Mrs. Banks. She'll be expecting y'u. Mi names Carter. Follow me."

Sophie's heels clicked loudly on the wooden floor. Maids and footmen whizzed passed her, heat poured out of a busy kitchen, followed by a booming, angry voice. Sophie stopped, terrified, as her heart jumped into her throat. She wanted to run away back to Derby, to all the familiar things she loved.

"'ere we are." Carter tapped on the door marked Head Housekeeper.

"Come in." He opened the door.

"Miss Romano to see you, Mrs. Banks." Carter stepped to the side to allow Sophie to enter. She walked slowly into the small sitting room. Each step was taking her into a world she didn't know or understand.

"Thank you, Carter. Miss Romano, take a seat." Mrs. Banks stood up from the rocking chair by the fireplace and sat at the small round table, indicating for Sophie to join her. She poured tea from the tray on the table. Handing Sophie a cup and saucer, she smiled and Sophie relaxed.

"Miss Romano, I understand you have never worked as a maid. Mr. Dalton came to see me, explaining your circumstances and I am sorry for your loss." Mrs. Banks reached out, touching Sophie's hand. "I'll do whatever I can to help you. Mr. Dalton spoke highly of you. He said you worked in your father's office and also understood household management. The only position available in the hotel at this time is a junior maid's position—maid-of-work, usually filled by very young girls. The hours are long, the work is hard, the pay is low. But you can call The Sackville home."

"Thank you, Mrs. Banks. I'm sure I can do the work."

"If you are a fast learner and as the opportunities arise I can move you up to maid. Bring your things on Sunday, ready to start work at five Monday morning."

Sophie thanked Mrs. Banks and took the omnibus back to Hastings. She wondered when Dalton had been to see her. She smiled to herself, realizing his sister's friend who worked at The Sackville, was Dalton himself. She wondered what the connection was between him and Mrs. Banks. Just knowing there was a connection allowed her to feel safe or was it her naivete.

A new beginning for young innocent Sophie, her life of privilege gone. Alone in the world, she faced a life of drudgery as a humble maid at The Sackville Hotel. Her future looked bleak but her father had taught her well. His dream of her running the silk mill was not to be but with her own strength, and Alberto in her heart, she would find a way to thrive.

The prequel ends but Sophie's stories are just beginning.
Prelude to Sophie's War ... https://geni.us/MWT
Book one of the Sophie Books
The Blue Pendant https://geni.us/N6BQ
Book one of The Sackville Hotel Trilogy

Epilogue

ophie works hard and does well as a maid at The Sackville Hotel. After war breaks out and on the rebound from a lost love Sophie decided to serve her country as a nurse and joins the Bartley Hospital in London as a probationary nurse.

Acknowledgments

There is no greater sense of accomplishment for an author than placing the last period on the final page. But that period is only the beginning of a long process to turn a diamond in the rough into a sparkling jewel. The story writing part is solitary, the polishing part requires expertise from professionals. I am grateful for having a great team behind me. Many thanks to my daughter-in-law, Laura Cavaliere, and her sister Elisa Cavaliere, for re-writing my very poor Google-translated Italian and for the first edition editor Mark McGahey. My thanks go to Myriam McCormack and her dog Sammy—whose walks went off schedule while Myriam proofed and made sense of things that I had not. Kudos to the team at Tellwell.ca for both the original interior and cover design.

In 2022, I decided to revise this book as it is the prequel to not one, but two, of my series and it needed to reflect both books. This required a second edit after I had played with the words. My current editor, Meghan Negrijn, worked her magic as she always does. Thank you, Meghan. Always a pleasure. The original cover designed by Tellwell has been updated to reflect the two series mentioned above.

Snippets of Praise

Here are a few snippets of praise

The Blue Pendant - Amazon 5 star ratings around the world.

Sally from the U.K. said, *A brilliant read....I was totally engaged from the beginning to the very last page.....can't wait for the sequel..."*

Evelyn B, from the U.S. said, *"Unbelievable story – I loved it. Amazing book!!! Heartwarming and heartbreaking all at the same time...the history was spot on...Is there going to be a sequel?"*

Prelude to Sophie's War - Amazon average rating 4.5 star

Granny J from the UK - Really enjoyed this book. It is good to see Sophie's life story unfolding. Would recommend reading all the previous stories about Sophie.

Heart of Sophie's War - Amazon average rating 4.5 star

Sharon B - Very Good read

Enjoyed this book immensely as I did The Sackville Hotel Trilogy. I am looking forward to Book 3 in this series.

About the Author

Susan A. Jennings was born in Derby, England of a Canadian mother and English father. Drawn by her Canadian heritage, she settled in Ottawa, Canada, where she now lives and writes overlooking the Ottawa River. An essential element of her writing is weaving both British and Canadian cultures into her stories, notably prominent in The Sackville Hotel Trilogy. The Lavender Cottage novels are set in a quaint British village and the other historical novels, The Sophie's War Novels are set in London and Passchendaele during the first world war.

Susan lives with her dog Miss Penny, who has her own weekly blog

Miss Penny's Blog
https://susanajennings.com/blog

You can connect with me on:
🌐 https://susanajennings.com
🔲 https://facebook.com/authorsusanajennings

Subscribe to my newsletter:

✉ https://geni.us/NewsfromSusan

Also by Susan A Jennings

The Sackville Hotel Trilogy
   Book 1 - The Blue Pendant
   Book 2 - Anna's Legacy
   Book 3 - Sarah's Choice
   Box Set - All three books
   Prequel – Ruins in Silk*

Sophie's War Series
   Book 1 - Prelude to Sophie's War
   Book 2 - Heart of Sophie's War
   Book 3 - In the Wake of Sophie's War
   Prequel - Ruins in Silk *
   *Leads into The Blue Pendant and Sophie's War

The Lavender Cottage Books
   Book 1 - When Love Ends Romance Begins
   Book 2 - Christmas at Lavender Cottage
   Book 3 - Believing Her Lies
   Book 4 - Second Chances

Nonfiction
   Save Some for me - A Memoir
   A Book Tracking Journal for ladies
   Forget-Me-Not A Book Tracking Journal
   A Dog with a Blog - Miss Penny Speaking

Short Stories:
  Mr. Booker's Book Shop
  The Tiny Man
  A Grave Secret
  Gillian's Ghostly Dilemma
  The Angel Card
  Little Dog Lost Reiki Found

Story Collections
  The Blue Heron Mysteries
  Contributing author to:
  The Black Lake Chronicles
  Ottawa Independent Writers' Anthologies

Printed in Great Britain
by Amazon

26753584R00098